Root Beer Candy and Other Miracles

Root Beer

Candy and Other Miracles

SHARI GREEN

pajamapress

First published in Canada and the United States in 2016

www.pajamapress.ca info@pajamapress.ca

 Canada Council Conseil des arts
for the Arts du Canada

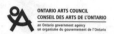 ONTARIO ARTS COUNCIL
CONSEIL DES ARTS DE L'ONTARIO
an Ontario government agency
un organisme du gouvernement de l'Ontario

 Canada

The publisher gratefully acknowledges the support of the Canada Council for the Arts and the Ontario Arts Council for its publishing program. We acknowledge the financial support of the Government of Canada through the Canada Book Fund (CBF) for our publishing activities.

Library and Archives Canada Cataloguing in Publication

Green, Shari, 1963-, author
    Root beer candy and other miracles / Shari Green.

ISBN 978-1-77278-007-9 (paperback)

    I. Title.

PS8613.R4283R66 2016   jC813'.6   C2016-901339-1

Publisher Cataloging-in-Publication Data (U.S.)

Names: Green, Shari, author.
Title: Root beer candy and other miracles / Shari Green.
Description: Toronto, Ontario Canada : Pajama Press, 2016. | Summary: "Sent to an island town to stay with her estranged grandmother while her parents try to save their crumbling marriage, 11-year-old Bailey feels helpless and cast away. When a self-proclaimed prophet predicts "a stranger from the sea will change everything," Bailey hopes this stranger can solve her problems – little suspecting her own ability to influence the world" -- Provided by publisher.
Identifiers: ISBN 978-1-77278-007-9 (paperback)
Subjects: LCSH: Family problems – Juvenile fiction. | Grandparent and child – Juvenile fiction. | Friendship – Juvenile fiction. | Novels in verse | BISAC: JUVENILE FICTION / Family / Multigenerational. | JUVENILE FICTION / Family / Marriage & Divorce. | JUVENILE FICTION / Social Themes / Friendship.
Classification: LCC PZ7.5G744Roo |DDC [Fic] – dc23

Cover illustration—François Thisdale
Sea shells—©Hein Nouwens/Shutterstock
Cover design—Rebecca Buchanan
Interior design and typesetting—Rebecca Buchanan and Martin Gould

Manufactured by Friesens
Printed in Canada

Pajama Press Inc.
181 Carlaw Ave., Suite 207, Toronto, Ontario Canada, M4M 2S1

Distributed in Canada by UTP Distribution
5201 Dufferin Street, Toronto, Ontario Canada, M3H 5T8

Distributed in the U.S. by Ingram Publisher Services
1 Ingram Blvd., La Vergne, TN 37086, USA

For Lisa

OUR LADY OF THE BAY

After the storm
Felicity Bay is washed clean—
cottage roofs rain-fresh,
gleaming
in the morning sun.
I lean over the porch railing,
scan the ribbon
of wet sand.
Last night's wind rearranged driftwood
along the beach
like my mother scrubbing,
dusting,
moving furniture around
after she and Dad fight.
My brother couldn't sleep.
This morning I found him
on Nana Marie's ocean-blue couch,
wrapped in a sheet.

Nana Marie calls me inside
before I can explore.

Bailey, she hollers. *Pancakes.*

I kick off my flip-flops,
dash in,
plop down across from Kevin
at the kitchen table.

> *Don't just stare at them,* Nana Marie says.
> *Eat, Chickadee.*

> *She has to check them first,* says Kevin.

He thinks it's dumb
that I study the gold and white designs
fried into flapjacks,
searching
for the face of God.
He was only little
when Aunt Debbie discovered Tom Hanks
staring at her
from her breakfast plate.
She watched every one of his movies
after that,
said it changed her life.
So I say,
> *You never know,*
and I check for God.

Later that morning
I find Daniel outside,
peering at things
through his camera.

Beep
click
beep.

He turns on the camera,
snaps a picture,
turns it off.

Daniel's eleven,
same as me.
He stays in the cottage
next to Nana Marie's
and takes pictures
of everything.

       Where ya going? Daniel says.

       Nowhere, I say,
and we start going there
together.

A short trail cuts through beach grass—
gray-green blades
as long as my legs,
dancing
in the breeze.
Daniel and I leap
onto silvery driftwood logs.

We're surfing,
skateboarding,
teetering
on a balance beam.
If we touch the sand
it's one point against us.
Daniel always loses
because he jumps down to snap photos
of things I don't see.

Beep
click
beep.

My brother's not really a fan
of the beach—
he'd rather hunt for bugs
or stay inside to read comics,
so I'm glad
I know Daniel.
Already it feels
like we've been friends
a long time.

We're halfway around the bay
when I see her.
        Look, I say,
taking another point against me
so I can sprint over
and examine her close-up.
        A driftwood mermaid. See?

Daniel's face scrunches up,
and I know he thinks
it's just a twisted
old
log.

   No, really, I say,
and I point out her tail,
run my hand up the smooth curve
of her neck.
   This is her head.

Daniel shrugs
then walks a little farther
down the beach.
He comes back with a handful
of dark blonde kelp,
stretches up,
arranges it on the wood
the way the lady at SuperCuts
fluffs my hair around my shoulders,
trying to make it behave
after she trims it.

   Now, he says,
   it looks like a mermaid.

A shiver tickles my neck
and ripples
down my spine.

She's special—I know it.
A gift from the ocean,
carried on the waves by last night's storm
so she and I could meet.

Daniel's not even looking at her,
just digging around in the sand
and snapping pictures.
But then he walks up,
        says, *Hold out your hand,*
and onto my palm
he drops a piece of sea glass,
edges worn smooth,
brilliant turquoise—
the very same turquoise
I imagine a mermaid's tail
would be.

We christen her *Our Lady of the Bay.*
I curtsey,
nudge Daniel with my elbow
so he'll bow.
Then we run toward the sea,
jump waves
till we're soaked with salt water
and laughter.

CREAMSICLES

Daniel, Kevin, and I
wander the boardwalk,
watch tourists on their way to the beach
struggling with inner tubes,
buckets,
towels,
and little kids.

Seeing all those families
pinches my heart.
My parents should be here.
We should be together,
the four of us—
diamonds, clubs, spades, hearts,
Crazy Eights on a Sunday afternoon,
four quarters making a whole
like we always used to be
but might never be
again.

A cart clatters along the boards—
half freezer,
half bicycle,
driven by a white-haired man.

Jasper Angelopoulos, Daniel tells me.
He used to be the preacher
at that old church.

Daniel jerks his head
to point down the boardwalk.
A block away, white steeple
meets blue sky.

Got kicked out or something, Daniel says.
Now he has that ice cream cart.
Rides up and down the boardwalk
every day in summer—
except Tuesdays, of course.

Tuesdays it rains
in Felicity Bay.
Nobody wants ice cream
when it's raining.

Kevin eyeballs the cart
as it approaches.
Before we left the cottage,
Nana Marie told me
to watch out for Kevin
because he's only eight.

She doesn't know
I don't need a reminder,
doesn't know that back home
I let him sleep in my room
when Mom and Dad fight,
and rescue his school lunch
after the Harris twins
steal it.

     Hey Kev, I say now. *Want a Popsicle?*

     Fudgsicle! Kevin says.

Jasper stops his cart beside us.
He smiles,
and the wrinkles in his tanned face
deepen
into trenches.

While we're buying our treats,
Daniel's big brother shows up.
Levi watches out for Daniel
like I do for Kevin,
even though Daniel's too old
to need watching.
Levi's the last
to get his ice cream.
Jasper hands him a Creamsicle
but doesn't let go,
just stares at Levi,
starts talking with a voice deep and slow,

a river that's not in any hurry
to get
where it's going.

> *It will come to pass*
> *that a stranger*
> *from the sea*
> *will change*
> *everything.*

He smiles again,
hands over the Creamsicle,
hops on his half freezer, half bicycle
and rides away.

> *What was that about?* I ask.

> *Nothing,* Levi says. *Crazy old Jasper*
> *thinks he's a prophet, is all.*
> *Thinks he knows the future.*

I don't say anything
but I think,
how do you know
he's *not* a prophet?
And also,
what
if
he
is?

A SPOON OF SIGNIFICANCE

We're going out to celebrate,
says Nana Marie.

Two weeks ago,
Kevin and I said goodbye to Mom and Dad,
sailed to Arbutus Island,
watched dolphins play
in the wake of the ferry.
Waiting for us was a grandmother
we barely knew.
Now we know her,
and now
she wants to celebrate.

Kevin asks if Mom and Dad are coming
even though he knows
they're still at camp.
They're spending a month
at Marriage Repair.
Mom said it was a retreat, but I picture it
like summer camp—

stuck in a canoe, learning
to work together,
remembering not to hide secrets
like candy wrappers
the counselor will find under your bed
during cabin inspection,
ending each day
with campfire songs
and cocoa.

I tell Kevin no,
it'll be at least
two more weeks.
His chin juts out.

I don't even care, he says.

Nana Marie and Kevin and I
stroll to Marina Grill.
From our table on the patio
we watch boats coming and going,
gulls circling,
diamonds sparkling
on the water.
The smell of fried fishy goodness
tangles
with delicious sea air,
tickling my nose.
I order halibut and chips.

Kevin chooses boring grilled cheese
like always,
and Nana Marie only orders
ice cream.

    No dinner? I ask.

    Life's short, she says, *and I'm old.*

When the waiter brings our food,
he slaps down a big dish of vanilla
with chocolate sauce
and peanuts
for Nana Marie.
When I see it, I think of Jasper
and his ice cream cart,
and what he said to Levi.
I keep thinking on it
while I'm eating,
gulls squawking non-stop behind me
interrupting
my thoughts.
Jasper's words feel important,
but I can't grab hold
of why.

The warm breeze lifts my napkin,
sends it fluttering
to the floor.

Finally, I tell Nana Marie
about the prophecy—
how Jasper said a stranger from the sea
would change things.
Nana Marie gazes at the water,
lets out a small sigh.

> *He's at it again, is he?* she says.

> *Is that a bad thing?*

Nana Marie looks back at me,
takes her time
deciding on an answer.

> *I hope not, she says.*
> *But last time he got serious*
> *about the voice-of-God thing,*
> *it didn't end well.*
> *He upset a lot of people.*
> *Got himself in trouble*
> *with the church.*

> I say, *Why would the church get mad*
> *about hearing the voice of God?*

> *Perhaps*, says Nana Marie,
> scooping up the last bite
> of her sundae,

they didn't believe it was
the voice of God. Or perhaps they did,
but they didn't like
what God had said.
Or, she says, *perhaps*
they just didn't want to believe
it was coming from Jasper.

She licks her spoon,
wipes it
on a napkin,
drops it
into her purse.

Kevin's eyes bug out.
He opens his mouth
but I squash my own giggle
and shush him
before he has a chance to blurt out
anything.
My mother would never believe
that *her* mother
snitched a spoon—
or maybe
she would. Maybe
there's a reason
Nana Marie was last
on Mom's where-to-send-us
list.

Back at the cottage,
Nana Marie sticks a hand in her purse,
fishes around blindly
like the men who stand on the pier
dropping lines into the sea,
hoping to hook
a big one.
When she comes up
with Marina Grill's spoon,
she jams it into a spot
on a display rack
nearly full
of mismatched teaspoons.

    Isn't that for souvenir spoons? I say.
    Little ones?

    These are souvenirs, she says,
    pulling out one from the middle.
    From Denny's,
    the day I moved to Felicity Bay
    to live year-round—
    first big decision I made
    after your Grandpa Harold died.

She lifts another spoon
from the rack,
cradles it in her hands
for me and Kev to admire.

From Agnes Creelman's
special-company-only
silverware set.
It was quite an honor.
Agnes doesn't pull out the good stuff
for just anyone, you know.

Maybe we don't know Nana Marie all that well—
not yet. But one thing's clear.
She's not
just
anyone.

BOBBING

The beach is empty
this early in the day.
Later when it's hot,
the sand will be cluttered—
colorful towels,
picnic coolers,
kids building castles with moats.
Now it's just me and the gulls.
A huge crowd of them
squawk and screech
when I get too close,
take off in a frenzy of flapping
then land again
a short distance away.
I scan the waves,
hoping
for dolphins
but not seeing any.
Maybe they're all still chasing
the ferry.

I wish I could wade in,
dunk my head,
dive
under the surface,
but Nana Marie's rule
is No Swimming Alone.
She wouldn't come with me,
says she doesn't ever swim.
It's not because she's old—
she acts way younger
than other grandmas I know—
so I don't get it.
How can she live by the beach
and not go in the water?
Kevin didn't want to come, either.
When I left the cottage,
he and Nana Marie were elbow-deep
in a bin of LEGO.

They don't know
what they're missing.
Even if I can't go swimming
until Daniel gets here,
there's still wet sand
for cartwheels,
shallow tide pools
for exploring,
until the ocean
sneaks back to the shore
and swallows it all.

I crouch down,
turn over a rock,
watch little green crabs scurry
for new hiding places.
They remind me of Kevin
pulling the covers over his head
when Mom and Dad fight,
tugging his ball cap low
when he rides the bus.

When a wave washes over my feet
Jasper's words
wash over my brain.

A stranger from the sea

The water pulls back,

will change everything—

swishes over my toes,

a stranger

slides back again.

from the sea.

I straighten up,
shade my eyes from morning sun
like a sailor searching
the horizon. Land ho!
I run,
bare feet slapping wet sand
until my chest is about to burst open
and there she is—*Our Lady of the Bay*.
A stranger
from the sea.

I *knew* she was special.

I race back,
zigging
        zagging
to avoid seashells,
tide pools,
mounds of seaweed
on the sand.
Up to the path—
no shoes!
Where are my shoes?
Doesn't matter,
keep dashing
to Daniel's.

I pound on the door.

    Hurry, Daniel. She's magic!

The door opens,
a face
pokes out.

Hey, Bailey.

It's Levi,
Daniel's brother.

Who's magic? he says.

I don't want to tell him.
He's almost fifteen—
probably too old
to believe in magic.

I need to see Daniel, I say.

He's not done with his treatments.

The door's wide open now:
Levi in shorts and t-shirt,
bare feet on sandy hardwood,
a bowl of cereal in his hands.

Treatments? I ask.

For his lungs. Maybe an hour still.

I don't know why lungs
would need treatments.
Lungs are supposed to work
on their own.

      You can wait if you want, Levi says.
      We should stay out here, though.
      My dad's still sleeping—
      came over on the last ferry
      yesterday after work.

Levi brings out another bowl,
box of cereal,
jug of milk.
We sit on the porch,
don't talk,
just eat
and watch the ocean.
I swirl my spoon
through the cereal,
colorful loops bobbing
in a pink sea,
tangled thoughts bobbing
in my head.
After a long while
      I ask, *Have you seen the mermaid?*

Levi's brow furrows, and heat
rushes to my face.

The driftwood, I say. *It looks
like a mermaid.*

If he's too old
to see magic,
he probably can't see mermaids
either.

Levi refills his bowl,
holds out the box
            —want some more?—
shakes another pile
into my bowl.

            So, you like it here? Levi asks.

            I love it, I say,
but after the words hit the air
they turn back,
punch me
in the stomach.
I'm only here
because of marriage camp.
I'm only here
because my family
is broken.
I *do* love this island—
the beach,
the salty air,
getting to know Nana Marie,
making friends with Daniel—

but I would trade it all
if it would keep Mom and Dad
together.
Last time Mom phoned us
to check in,
she said camp was fine,
Dad was fine,
she was fine,
but I think *fine*
is code for *I don't want*
to talk about it.

I need to think
of something else.

   Maybe he's almost done, I say.

   Yeah, Levi says, *not long now.*

He slurps milk from his bowl,
wipes a drip
off his chin.

   What sort of treatments, anyway?

   Medicines, Levi says. *Lots of them.*
   And chest physio.
   It clears out his lungs.

   Fixes them?

Levi shakes his head.

> *No, just helps him breathe.*
> *You can't fix them.*

How does Daniel
run
swim
talk
breathe
with broken lungs?
And what if the treatments
don't work?

The door creaks open
but no one
appears.

Beep
click
beep.

Daniel is on his stomach
in the doorway,
camera in his hands pointed
toward the colorful box
by Levi's feet.
He grins up at me.
I smile back, but only
on the outside.

Inside, I'm thinking how so much
is broken.
I'm thinking how so much
needs to be
changed.

Bailey: I'm glad you're here.

Our Lady Of The Bay: Me, too. It's lovely here.

Bailey: I mean, I'm glad you came from the sea to change everything.

OLOTB: Have you ever wondered about sand? It's really quite amazing.

Bailey: What? No, I—can we talk about how you're going to fix things? How you're going to change them? I mean, maybe miracles have to be secret right up until they happen. I get that, but just a hint?

OLOTB: I don't get to spend much time sitting on dry sand, you know, but I'm rather enjoying it. Some might say I'm stuck here—beached, as it were—but it's really quite a nice change.

Bailey: Speaking of changes…

OLOTB: You should look at it under a microscope.

Bailey: Look at what?

OLOTB: The sand. You'd think it would be boring bits of gray nothingness, but it's not. It's minerals—quartz, fragments of sea shells, all sorts of delightful things. Exquisite, really.

Bailey: So, I just ran across a bunch of minerals?

OLOTB: Who'd have thought you were tromping on such beauty?

ROOT BEER CANDY

The ice cream cart
of Jasper Angelopoulos
is parked
outside the market.
Kevin and I follow Nana Marie inside,
ducklings trailing
after their mama.
The store is crowded with goods—
boxes and tins overflowing the shelves
into piles on the floor,
as if the room was once larger
and the walls closed in,
squeezing everything closer together.

Mama Duck claims a basket,
shoos us over to the till
where penny candy waits.

> *Get yourselves some sugar,* she says
> with a wink. *I'm serving nothing but vegetables*
> *from here on, so you'd best stock up.*

We zip over
to check out the selection—
hard candy sticks in every color,
bins of jelly beans
to scoop into paper bags,
bubble gum and caramels,
jelly worms and jawbreakers,
and a glass jar stuffed full
of giant blue lollipops.
My mouth waters
at the sight of all that *yum*,
and Kevin's practically drooling.
I pass him one of the little bags,
remind him to decide
before touching.

> *I know!* says Kevin.
> *I'm not a baby.*

Jasper walks up to the counter
holding a loaf of bread.
He smiles at us,
nods his head
toward the candy.

> *Try the root beer ones,* he says.
> *They're the best.*

I want to ask him
about the prophecy—
if it really and truly was
about the mermaid.
I want to ask about magic
and miracles,
how a driftwood stranger
from the sea
can change everything.
Instead I just smile back,
watch him stack coins
one on top of the other
to pay for his bread.

As he leaves the store
I turn back to the sweets,
choose Double-Bubble
and striped candy sticks—
strawberry,
butterscotch,
and root beer.

A voice comes from behind me.

> *If he's going to start*
> *all that prophet nonsense again,*
> *he ought to move somewhere*
> *people want to hear it.*

I turn around,
see two ladies in flowery sundresses,
shopping baskets in hand,
lurking
by a stack of laundry detergent.
They must be talking
about Jasper.
They must've heard
about what he said to Levi.
I wonder if they know
about the mermaid.

He's hardly a prophet, one lady says.
*I don't know why he thinks
he's so special.*

I take a look
through the store window,
watch Jasper put his bread
in with the Creamsicles,
Fudgsicles,
Popsicles,
and pedal away,
not looking like he thinks he's
particularly special
at all.

You ready, Chickadee?

For a moment
the way Nana Marie's looking at me
from beside the front counter
reminds me of Mom.
They don't really look much alike
except for the hair—
light brown
with a little gray for Mom
and a lot
for Nana Marie—
but just now I can see
they're family.
My eyes prickle.

Nana Marie pays for our candy
and the basket of groceries—
a rainbow of colors
heaped
by the pot-of-gold cash register.
She wasn't kidding
about the vegetables.
It looks like we're in for meals
of peppers,
carrots,
and all manner
of leafy greens.

Out on the boardwalk,
outside *The Clam Shell*
where tourists buy sunglasses,
Felicity Bay t-shirts,
tiny *Gone to the Beach* flip-flop magnets,
several people are clustered
around Jasper's cart.
It looks like he drove
into a mob
of grandmothers.

As we approach the group,
Jasper's river voice
flows.
My feet stop moving
so my ears
can listen better.

> *It will come to pass*
> *that one treasure*
> *will be lost*
> *and a greater one*
> *found.*

Then Jasper's cart
carries him away
down the boardwalk.
Nana Marie stops to chat
with the ladies,
shifting the grocery bag from one hip
to the other.

What do you think it means?
says a lady even older
than Nana Marie.

You believe him? says another one.

Of course I do, says the extra-old lady.
He's a man of God.

Nana Marie shakes her head
as we turn to leave.

Oh dear, she mutters.

For a moment,
I worry *oh dear what?*
but then Jasper's words
bump out the thought,
and I think of treasure
lost
and found.
All the way back
to Nana Marie's cottage
I wonder what treasure has to do
with mermaids
or miracles
and if it's maybe
possibly
true

that *Our Lady of the Bay*
can help Mom and Dad
work things out.
It doesn't make sense
but sometimes
the most wonderful things
don't.

I pull a candy stick
from my bag,
peel back the wrapper,
pop the end
in my mouth.

Jasper was right:
a hint of mint
and vanilla,
and something spicy
that wakes up
the back of my tongue—
the root beer ones
really are
the best.

FALLING, SLIDING, LEAPING

Tuesday it rains
of course—
a perfect day
for books.
I've barely touched
the stack I brought to read,
so busy
on the beach.
I choose the one
about a gorilla
who can paint.

When I open the cover,
the picture I use as a bookmark
slips
to my lap—
Mom and Dad
huddled together beside a campfire,
smiling at me.
It's from two summers ago
when I still thought
things were okay.

My fingers trace the line of Mom's arm
to where her hand
joins Dad's.
Missing-them rushes through me,
tries to close my throat.
I swallow it down.

I prop the photo
on the dresser Kevin and I share,
then tuck a pillow
behind my back,
turn
to page one.

> *I'm bored,* Kevin says.

> *Read a book,* I say.

> *I already read six today.*

> *You need longer books.*

I look away
from the gorilla story,
see Kevin's face—
eyes wide
and hopeful,
like a puppy
saying please-oh-please-can-we-play.

Fine, I say. *Go pick*
a game.

Kevin races
to the living room
where Nana Marie keeps board games
piled
under an end table.
I tuck away my book
for later.
Nana Marie joins us.
She sits on the ocean-blue couch,
spins the dial,
calls out colors and body parts
while Kevin and I twist
like human pretzels.
I'm taller
and can almost do the splits,
but Kevin's bendier.
It's me who falls first
every time.

After Twister
we play Snakes and Ladders.
It seems whenever one of us
moves ahead,
gets close,
a snake comes along
and ruins everything.

After lunch, the rain still pounds
on the porch roof,
flattens wildflowers
and sea grass,
overflows the cottage gutters,
splatters
into sandy puddles.
I leave Kevin in our fort
on the porch
with Nana Marie's stack
of *Archie* comics
which you'd think she bought
just for us
but I suspect
not.

In the kitchen
Nana Marie is baking cookies—
containers of oatmeal,
brown sugar,
chocolate chips
scattered
across the counter.

> *Stir, Chickadee. My hands*
> *are finished.*

I take over mixing.
Baking is a kind of magic, really:
all sorts of ingredients,
some not very tasty—

flour, baking powder,
raw eggs,
yuck!—
but they come together
in a big old ceramic bowl
and *poof!*
something good.

I snitch a bit of dough
when it's ready.

> *This tastes the same*
> *as Mom makes,* I say.

> *Well, Miss Bailey,* says Nana Marie.
> *Who do you think taught your mom*
> *to make cookies?*

I try to imagine Mom
when she was little,
standing on a chair,
helping Nana Marie
with the stirring.

> *Why don't we see you much,*
> *Nana Marie?*
> *Why don't you and Mom*
> *ever talk?*

Nana Marie wipes up flour dust
and sugar,
runs a cloth over the counter
even after it's clean.

> *Things change, Chickadee.*
> *Some relationships*
> *are difficult.*

Things changed
with Mom and Dad.
What if they stop talking
to each other?
What if they decide
apart
is easier
than together?

I ask Nana Marie if she believes
in magic
or miracles,
if she thinks that's what it will take
for marriage camp to work,
for the learning,
trying,
remembering,
to make something good
between Mom and Dad again.

I don't know much about miracles,
says Nana Marie, *but I think*
we'll go to church on Sunday.

That's not much of an answer.

Maybe not, she says.
But maybe.

Next day a bunch of us—
Kevin and me and Daniel,
Levi and his two friends—
we all go up to the point,
crunching over a trail
of old leaves
already dried out again
by the August sun.
We kick up island smells—
arbutus,
cedar,
meadow grass—
to mix with the sea air.
An easy climb
puts us on top of a bluff.
Land falls away on one side
but the roots of an arbutus tree
dig deep,
holding the hill
together.

We survey our kingdom:
the whole ocean,
or at least
the whole bay.
We hope to spy seals or dolphins
but see only boats
wandering lazily
across the blue.

Levi reaches out,
takes hold of the rope dangling
from a hefty branch,
and leaps.
He swings over the water,
drops,
splashes,
sinks.
Then he pops up again,
whooping for joy.

His friends go next—
two guys that look so much the same
they might be twins.
First one swings,
drops.
Second one swings,
drops.
Daniel swings,
drops,

then Levi's back on the bluff,
herding me
toward the edge.

> *Come on, Bailey,* he says.
> *You're up.*

My stomach
is what's up.
I peer over the edge,
imagine clutching the rope,
tumbling
through the air,
plunging
into the depths.

> *I don't think Nana Marie*
> *would like me leaping*
> *into the sea.*

Levi waggles his eyebrows.

> *Your nana's not here,*
> *is she? Come on—go for it!*

I take a step backward.
Levi's friends reappear beside him,
antsy to grab the rope
and jump again.

You going? one says to me.

Yeah, Bailey, says the other.
You going? Or are you
chicken?

A clucking noise
comes from Thing One
and Thing Two,
taunting me.
Levi's two friends
are no friends
of mine.
Levi punches Thing One
in the arm,
      says, *Aw, just leave her be.*

      Bailey, says Kevin from behind me,
      I need to go back
      to Nana Marie's.

My stomach
is glad to hear it.

      I'll take you, I say,
just as a dripping-wet
coughing
Daniel
rejoins us
on the bluff.

He spits in the bush,
coughs again,
clears his throat
as he takes his place
in the line.
I'm not sure his lungs
want him to jump again,
but he's beaming,
eager
for his turn.

I hope he knows
what he's doing.

I watch Daniel
for another moment
then turn away,
abandoning the rope—
plus Thing One
and Thing Two.

Kevin and I
walk side by side
along the path,
retracing our steps
through the leaves.

Thanks, I tell him.

For what?

For not clucking.

I hear hooting and hollering behind us,
a splash,
laughter,
but I don't look back.

> *You didn't really need to leave,* I say.
> *Did you?*

Kevin shrugs.

A smile
stretches my face
and I nudge his shoulder.
He bumps me back,
grinning.

> *Race you home!* Kevin says.

He takes off
but for a moment
I'm stuck on the spot
because *home* doesn't mean Mom and Dad—
not here,
not while they're still away
at marriage camp.
A lump
rises in my throat.

I get the feeling our family
is swinging on a rope
above nothing,
and I wonder…
if Mom and Dad let go
do all of us
fall?

SUPERHEROES

The next day I wake up early,
tip-toe
to the living room,
climb aboard the ocean-blue couch,
and get lost
in my book.
I love how a story changes
when I read it—
words on paper
becoming something magical,
something that makes me feel better,
like Clark Kent
stepping into a phone booth,
transforming
into something powerful
to rescue me.

An animal snarls,
grabs my neck—
book falls,
      heart leaps!
I whirl around.

Kevin,
of course.

He's grinning wildly,
beach-towel cape draped
over his Spider-Man pajama shirt.

> *That's not funny,* I say.

> *Yes, it is.*

> *I don't think Spider-Man wears a cape.*

> *Spider-Man doesn't,*
> *but Super-Secret-Spider-Man does.*

> *And what does Super-Secret Spider-Man do*
> *besides attack innocent people*
> *while they're reading?*

> *Secret stuff.*
> *He spies—you know, SPYder-Man.*

> *He must be brave*
> *if he dares to spy on his big sister.*

I glare at him,
point to my eyes,
> say, *I have death-ray eyeballs, you know.*

Kevin screams
and tackles me.
We fall off the couch,
thud
on the floor,
laughing and screeching
till Nana Marie appears
in her housecoat,
shoos us out to the porch
while she makes breakfast.

After we eat
and help with dishes,
Kevin hauls out the LEGO bin
and I go for a walk,
passing the time
until Daniel can come out.
I wander the boardwalk,
turn down a side street,
see Jasper crouching
beside someone's front gate.

When I get closer I can see
he's unscrewing the hinges.
A nameplate on the gate
says *Angelopoulos*
in faded blue paint.

> *You're taking down your fence?* I say.

Got enough things
keeping people apart
without adding a crooked fence.

He goes back to work
on the hinge.

Then again, he says,
Harold would've said I should fix it—
would've called it a good
learning opportunity.

Harold? You mean
my Grandpa Harold?

The very same.
He was a fine carpenter.
But me? I'm not exactly handy
with a hammer.
I did help put the porch
on Harold and Marie's house, though.

Jasper helped build Nana Marie's porch?

He chuckles.

Just look for the boards
with dents smashed into them
from the hammer.
Those'll be the ones
I put in.

Jasper yanks a board
from the fence,
taps the nails out
with a hammer.

Do you miss Harold? I ask.

He gathers the bent nails
and drops them
in a soup can.

Yes, he says, *I sure do.*
It's always hard
to lose a friend.

I reach down,
pick a nail from the lawn,
add it to the can.

I lost a friend once—
she moved away with her mom
when her parents split up.

You must miss her.

Yeah. But mostly
I'm kind of mad at her.

For moving?

She could've stayed in town
with her dad
but she picked her mom.
She picked leaving.

Jasper goes to work
on the next board.

Sometimes people leave, he says.
Doesn't mean
they don't love us.

Sure it does—
if they could stay
but they don't.

It's not always as simple
as it looks.

That's what my parents say.

As Jasper knocks out nails,
more words
well up inside me,
like they've needed saying
for a long while
and were just waiting
for the right ears
to hear them.

I don't know what to do.
I've tried everything—
making dinner for them, with candles
and stuff,
getting them to tell me the story
of when they met,
sending love notes they think
are from each other
but are actually
from me—
but they still needed
marriage camp.

Jasper nods,
letting me know he's listening
as he works.

I'm not so sure marriage camp
will do the trick.

Jasper examines the board,
tosses it
into the pile.

Jasper, do you believe in miracles?

Sure I do.

And it's God who does miracles, right?

*I expect so. Except for the times
someone else does them
on God's behalf.*

I can't imagine
doing God-work.

Sounds like superhero stuff, I say,
reminding myself of Kevin.
*My brother likes to pretend
he's a superhero.*

Maybe he really is one, says Jasper.

He hasn't seen Kevin
with bed-head
and a beach-towel cape.

Maybe you are, too, he says.

That's just silly.

*I suppose that depends
on your definition
of a superhero.*

I hope *Our Lady of the Bay*
is a superhero.
I hope *she* can do God-work—
help my parents stay in love,

keep my family together,
and even
make Daniel's lungs work better.
I don't know how,
but somehow
I think she'll change things,
like the prophecy said.
I think she'll fix
everything.

She's *got* to.

RUNGS (AND LUNGS)

There's an old tree house
behind Daniel's cottage.
He didn't build it,
just patched it up
a couple summers ago
with Levi.
It still needs some fixing.
Climbing the ladder
always scares me a little—
crooked boards
fastened to the tree trunk,
some of them wobbling
when I step on them.
I holler to see if he's up there,
then grab hold,
take a deep breath,
and climb.

Just as my eyes
reach floor level—

beep
click
beep—

Daniel snaps a picture
of the top half of my head.
He's sitting
on the plank floor
grinning.
As I hoist myself
into the tree house
Daniel laughs,
stretches out a hand
to help me.

> *We need a handle*, I say.
> *Something*
> *to grab onto.*

In my mind I see Jasper's gate
leaning against the post,
a silver handle
in need
of a new home.

> *I bet I know where we can get one,*
> *and some boards, too,*
> *that we can cut up and use—*
> *better than those lousy things*
> *you call a ladder.*

We decide to go see if Jasper
will give us some supplies,
so before I even sit down
I'm back on that awful ladder.

> *If you hate the ladder,* Daniel says,
> *you could just jump down.*

Then he leaps
from the tree house,
lands
on the carpet of fir needles.
My mouth drops open.

> *You're crazy,* I say,
and he laughs.

By the time we get to Jasper's,
the pile of wood has grown
and the fence
has shrunk.
We tell him about the tree house.

> *Take whatever you need,* he says.

He finds his screwdriver
so we can salvage the handle
off the gate.

We lug the supplies
back to Daniel's,
drop them
under the tree house,
a cloud of dust rising
from the ground.
Daniel starts to cough—
has a major fit
can't stop
coughing
hacking
gasping
on and on
worse
than any cold or sickness
I've ever had.

My insides tighten
like a clenched fist.

        Should I get your mom? I ask,
voice raised to be heard
over the coughing.

Daniel shakes his head,
finally stops
after forever,
wipes his eyes
and spits
into the bush.

Are you okay?

Yeah, Daniel says. *I'll be fine.*

Daniel, what exactly is wrong
with your lungs?

I've got cystic fibrosis, he says.

Cystic fi—what?

Cystic fibrosis. I've got gunk
in my lungs. Clogs them up
so I cough.

Gunk?

Mucus. He smirks. *Thick, slimy mucus.*

I feel myself grimace,
nose wrinkling up.

You don't like the word mucus?

Sounds gross, I say.

Daniel makes a face,
uses a goofy voice:

Mucus, mucus, mucus!

Ew! Disgusting.

I hope you're not planning
to be a doctor.

Not a chance, I say.
I'll probably be a counselor,
or a social worker like my uncle.
What about you?
What do you want to be?

Doesn't matter.

Sure it does.

He shrugs.

You have to decide sometime.

Daniel nudges the pile of boards
with his foot.

We should work on the ladder, he says.

Just tell me.
You must have some idea—
some job you'd like.

Fine. I want to be
a tree-house builder. Now can we please
get to work?

He climbs up the old ladder
to get his tools.
The top rung
cracks
splinters
breaks in two
when he steps on it.

POPSICLE COMMUNION

Sunday morning,
we sit in the middle
of the church,
stand to sing,
kneel to pray.
I listen and watch,
on the lookout
for the truth about miracles.

Kevin makes a paper airplane
from the program—
folds,
       unfolds,
folds again.
Nana Marie reaches into her purse,
trades him a peppermint Life Saver
for the airplane.

Reverend Davidson steps behind a table
at the front,
lifts a white cloth

to reveal bread,
juice,
a silver cup.
Nana Marie's hand finds mine
and latches on.
A moment later she leans in,
whispers
in my ear.

> *Your Grandpa Harold gave that cup*
> *to the church,* she says.

I'm about to whisper back,
tell her I think the cup
is pretty,
but she straightens up,
lips pressed together,
chin trembling
the tiniest bit.

Reverend Davidson and his helpers
serve Communion—
grape juice
and tiny squares of bread.
The organ music stops.
The room
and my heart
are draped
with a wondrous hush
like swimming under water.

Nana Marie says Communion
reminds us we're loved,
and it works, too,
settling over my shoulders
like a warm quilt
on a rainy night.
Maybe that's a miracle,
but it feels
like a mystery.

I bet if Jasper
was still the minister
he'd serve Popsicles instead.
It would still be Communion—
wouldn't it?—
if we were sharing the Popsicles
together.

After the service
we file to the back.

> *You two go on ahead,*
> says Nana Marie.

We leave her to chat,
step out into the salty air,
see Daniel leaning
against a lamppost,
eating a sandwich.

He tosses the last of it
on the ground.
Gulls shriek their delight,
thankful for a boy
with bread to share.

> *Let's go,* Daniel says.
> *Gotta show you something.*
>
> *What is it?* I say.
>
> *You'll see.*
>
> *But where are we going?*
>
> *To the beach!*

We hurry back into the church,
find Nana Marie,
tell her we're leaving.
Then we take off
down the boardwalk,
along the path,
and onto the sand,
farther and farther.
When I see it,
I stop short,
catching my breath
and staring.

It wasn't me, Daniel says
with a grin, *but I wish it was.*

Two big shells,
mismatched,
fastened with wire
to *Our Lady of the Bay*—
a bikini top
for the mermaid.
I bet it was Levi
poking fun,
or maybe
helping her look more
real.

Daniel and Kevin laugh,
race to the water,
lob stones at a bit of flotsam.
I sink down on the sand,
lean against the mermaid,
imagine the gentle pulse of waves
is her heartbeat—
slow
and steady,
reminding me
of a wondrous hush.
I feel communion again—
not the bread-and-juice part
but the remember-you're-loved part—

friends…
brothers…
grandmothers…
and I guess if there's love
somehow
things will be okay.

HIDE AND SEEK

At the pier
we drink iced tea from cans—
Daniel, Levi, Kevin, me,
leaning against the railing,
hair blowing
in the breeze.

There! I point.

A seal looks right at us,
ducks under a wave,
playing hide and seek.
We watch to see
where he'll pop up next.

Nana Marie's tai chi group
meets on the pier
like they do every Monday,
but instead of stretching,
slow-moving
grace,
today there's a ruckus.

Did you hear about Jasper? says a woman—
a flowery-sundress market woman.
Don't you see? 'One treasure will be lost.'
He couldn't have known!
It's a scheme. A scam.
He tells everyone it will go missing,
then he takes it himself
so we'll all believe
he's a prophet.

I'm sure that's not
what the prophecy was referring to,
says Nana Marie.

Of course it is,
says the woman.
And now it's missing.

I sidle up to Nana Marie,
        whisper, *What's missing?*

It's nothing, she says. *Never mind.*

But she said—

Just a rumor, Nana Marie says
with a hard look
at the sundress lady.

Then, more to herself
than to me, she mutters,

If I'd known
that's how they'd interpret it…

It's a fact, says the sundress lady.
The chalice
is missing.

I frown.

Chalice?

Nana Marie sighs.

The fancy silver cup, she says,
for communion.

Nuh-uh!
Someone stole
from the church?

Jasper did, says the sundress lady.

I think of Jasper—
his half freezer, half bicycle,
gentle smile,
Creamsicles,
and root beer candy.

He wouldn't do that, I say.

Sundress-lady
looks down her nose
at me.

> *How long*
> *have you known him?*

My voice is small.

> *Three weeks,* I say. *Almost.*

Her mouth twitches—
one-quarter smirk,
three-quarters bad taste.

> *I've known him twenty years,* she says.
> *Trust me—it was him.*

Nana Marie steps forward,
stands tall,
speaks in a no-nonsense voice
that's kind of scary
and kind of awesome.

> *This*
> *is*
> *ridiculous.*
> *Of course Jasper didn't take it.*
> *I've known him a long time, too,*
> *and I know he'd never steal*
> *from the church.*

Sundress-lady says,

> *I can think of one big reason he would.*
> *He was practically run out of the church,*
> *remember? Now he's out for revenge,*
> *wants to get*
> *them*
> *back.*

I want to tell her that's crazy talk,
but Nana Marie takes my hand,
Kevin's hand,
turns us around,
marches us away,
her face set
in an expression
I can't read.

That night when it's quiet,
I think of the ruckus,
the chalice,
the *one big reason*,
and I wonder if the crazy talk
isn't so crazy.
I climb out of bed,
find Nana Marie doing stretches
in the living room.

> *Did Jasper really get kicked out*
> *of the church?*

Nana Marie bends
to one side,
arm in the air.

He left the church by choice,
but honestly, people made sure
that staying wasn't really an option.

So, do you think he wanted revenge,
like that lady said?

Not for a minute.

Is he going to go
to jail?

Nana Marie straightens up,
looks at me
with furrowed brow.

Jasper has a good heart, Chickadee.

But if they think
he took it—

Regardless of anyone's suspicions, she says,
pink blotches blossoming
on her neck,
Reverend Davidson's not likely
to involve the police.

He's always preferred to let things work out
in the Lord's good timing.

Nana Marie pulls one foot up,
half cross-legged
even though she's standing.

It's late, she says.
You'd best get some sleep.

She clasps her hands
above her head,
closes her eyes.
I pad down the hallway,
crawl back into bed,
but thoughts and questions
keep poking my brain—
sundress ladies
and prophecies
and stealing
from the church.
It seems like the truth
is playing hide and seek.
I guess you never know where
it will pop up.

TREASURE HUNT

Two days later
Daniel arrives
on Nana Marie's porch,
shovels in hand,
camera case hanging
from his shoulder.

> *Come on,* he says.
> *We've got treasure to find.*

One treasure will be lost
and a greater one
found.
Is there treasure to find?
Do prophecies
come true?

The other day I was sure
things would work out
with my parents—
a miracle
would change everything.

No more arguing,
slamming,
leaving.
No more wondering
if I'll have to choose
Mom
or Dad.
But when they called last night,
crackly tension
crawled through the phone
from camp
to me.
My thoughts turned
like the tide,
and today, wishing for miracles
seems silly.

But…
what about those times
when the sun
sprinkles diamonds on the water,
or a seal
stares at me with big eyes?
Those times are real
but they feel
magical.
And maybe the bits of magic
in the world
really *are* miracles.
Maybe they're from God,
and if so,

it's not silly to think
a driftwood mermaid
could make a prophecy
come true.

I slide my feet into flip-flops,
claim a shovel,
grin at Daniel.
I know exactly
where to start searching
for treasure.

We dig holes knee-deep
around the mermaid,
creating mounds of sand
like haphazard castles.
When I strike something hard
we drop shovels,
scoop with hands,
hope for treasure
but find
a stone.
Daniel wants to try digging
in the churchyard
near the treasure
that was lost.

   We shouldn't, I say. *Isn't the ground*
   holy or something?

It will be, Daniel says,
after we've had a go at it.
Get it?
Hole-y?

He laughs until he coughs

and coughs

and coughs.

He doesn't want to go home,
says he's fine
but the coughing
puts me on edge.
   I say, *Maybe that's enough digging*
   for today.

We sit and stare
at the places we know
the treasure *isn't,*
pushing our feet beneath the sand,
letting it trickle
between our toes.
The sun warms our backs.

Beep
click
beep.

Our sandy toes wave
at the camera.

Even without treasure
today feels good,
like teamwork
and trying
and hope.

Daniel jumps up,
sand scattering.

> *We may not be good treasure hunters,* he says,
> *but we're good explorers—come on!*

I don't get up.

> *You sure you're okay?*
> *Maybe we shouldn't run around*
> *so much.*

He plants his fists
on his hips.

> *I'm on a soccer team, you know.*
> *I run all the time.*

We dash to Daniel's place first,
find his mom at the back of their cottage,
rinsing paintbrushes
under the tap.

A stripe of blue
stains her cheek.

We tell her we're going around the point
to the caves.

> *Be careful,* she says. *Stay together.*

Then we tell Nana Marie.
She took me and Kevin to the caves
the first week we were here.
Today she looks out at the sea,
purses her lips
as she contemplates
the tide.
The water is way out.
No way will we get stranded
in a sandstone cave.

Nana Marie nods.

> *Stay together,* she says.

Why do adults always think kids
are going to ditch each other?

> *Wear your hat,* Nana Marie adds.
> *You don't want sunstroke.*

Whatever that is,
I guess I don't want it,
so I grab my ball cap,
fidget
as Nana Marie slathers sunscreen
on the back of my neck,
and then we're off.

We walk the beach
from the sandy middle
to the pebbly curve,
all the way to the point
where the stones grow huge
and flatten out.
There are little holes scattered
across the rock—
bubbly
like the foam
that washes onto shore
with the waves
or like bubble wrap
that's all been
pop
pop
popped.

Around the tip of the point
another bay—
smaller
and wilder.

At high tide the ocean
can get pretty crazy,
big waves rushing into the bay.
Along the side
where Daniel and I skitter
across the rocks,
the wind and water and salt
carved out caves,
scooping away sandstone
a few grains at a time,
day after day,
year after year.

We walk along the edge,
the curved wall beside us
stretching up
and out,
hanging over our heads.
In one place
we find a window
in the sandstone wall
like a porthole looking through
to another world,
or at least
to the next cave.
Daniel zips to the other side
and we goof around,
pretend it's a mirror,
make faces
and copy each other's expressions.

We find a cubby hole
carved into the wall,
big enough for two kids
or maybe even three.

> *This is the coolest place,* I say.
> *Imagine a hundred years ago*
> *or a thousand years,*
> *the caves weren't even here,*
> *or if they were*
> *they were smaller,*
> *just dents in the stone.*

> *And imagine,* says Daniel,
> *how they'll be in fifty more years*
> *or a hundred more,*
> *after the salt water's had more time*
> *to work on them.*

I definitely want to see that.
An idea floods in.

> *Let's make a pact,* I say.
> *Let's promise to come back*
> *in fifty years.*
> *We'll meet in Felicity Bay*
> *and explore the caves*
> *when we're old.*

I hold up my hand,
baby finger extended.

Pinkie swear, I say.

Guys don't pinkie swear.

I open my hand flat.

Okay fine, I say.
Shake?

Daniel shrugs,
doesn't shake my hand.

It'll be great, I say.
Don't you want to?
We'll be ancient,
like Nana Marie,
but we can still come here.
We can still be explorers.

I won't be here, Daniel says.

We'll travel
from wherever we are.
And we'll meet again—
explorers reunited!

No, I mean…I probably
won't be alive.

People with cystic fibrosis
don't live that long.

The cubby hole seems to shrink,
and something inside me
gets washed away,
as if a hundred years of salt and wind and waves
rushed through me
all at once.

I find my voice.

Well, forty years, then.

He shrugs again.

Thirty?

He doesn't answer.
Tears prick at my eyes
so I look out at the bay—
muddy sand flats waiting
for the tide to return.

It's okay, says Daniel.

I look back at his face,
but he stands up
quick as a flash.

Tag, he says,
slapping my shoulder.
You're it.

He takes off,
leaping from bubble rock
to bubble rock,
laughing.

I chase after him
trying
not to cry.

THE TWIST

Felicity Bay celebrates
the town's birthday—
cake in the park,
lemonade,
Jasper handing out Popsicles
for free,
even to people
who are mad at him.
Everyone is there,
including tourists
and flowery-sundress ladies.

All us kids play Kick the Can
while the old folks dance
to a summer band.
When I'm waiting to be freed
after I'm caught,
I watch Nana Marie
do the twist.

Daniel starts coughing,
so we take a break
from the game,

find a picnic table
in the shade
of a cedar tree.
Jasper's ice cream cart
is parked under the tree.
After a while,
he comes over,
sits across from us,
asks if we're having fun.

Absolutely, I say.

Kevin wanders off
in search of bugs.
The band finishes playing,
and the dancing old folks
sink
into lawn chairs,
settle
into shade,
like us.
The park grows quiet,
townspeople and tourists
content,
full of cake
and music,

until...

That was nice, someone says,
'though not as nice
as last year.

Nana Marie clucks her tongue.

Agnes, she says, *just because* you
didn't organize it
doesn't mean
it wasn't grand. I think
it was grand.

You wouldn't know grand, says Agnes,
if it broke down your door
and stayed to dinner.

Nana Marie's face bunches up
like she's about to give Agnes
what for,
but a voice interrupts:

The band
was too loud, the cake
was too sweet.

Soon half the people in the park
are arguing
with the other half,
until finally
everyone stomps off
in different directions.

Back at the cottage
Nana Marie marches
across the kitchen, snatches
a souvenir spoon,
hurls it
in the garbage.

Special company my arse, she says.

I laugh
because she said *arse*
but then I see pink cheeks,
damp eyes,
hurt
more than anger,
and I realize it was the spoon
from her visit with Agnes.
I wrap my arms around her.

It wasn't always like this,
she says. *Used to be
we all got along,
and parties didn't deteriorate
into madness.*

I step back
from the hug.

Nana Marie shakes her head.

Sometimes I wonder
why I ever moved back here.

What happened? I ask.
What made it different?

I don't know,
but years ago
it was almost as if the water itself
made people happy.
They'd go into the sea
one person,
come out
another—
hurts, fears, anger
somehow washed away.
But then Jasper…
well, things changed.
And Harold—
he was a strong swimmer,
loved the water—
when the sea took him
people stopped swimming,
stopped trusting in the water
of Felicity Bay.
Seems like ever since then,
grudges and gossip build up
and never
get washed away.

I get thinking
about all the time
I've spent at the beach.
No one swimming
except tourists and kids
splashing around,
dunking,
wriggling like salmon
under the surface.
All of us
were happy.

What about
everyone else?

When Mom calls
after dinner,
I tell her about the good party
gone bad.
She says that can happen
to even the best
of things.

Bailey: Things are not going well.

OLOTB: No?

Bailey: I thought it was just my parents who needed help, and Daniel. But now it's Jasper and the whole town. Even the party turned bad—people were getting along and having fun, then all of a sudden it was like they forgot how to be happy.

OLOTB: That's a shame.

Bailey: I hope you're almost ready with the miracles.

OLOTB: Do you know what my favorite creatures are?

Bailey: …

OLOTB: Sea stars. I'm very fond of them. Can you guess why?

Bailey: Their colors?

OLOTB: They regenerate—if they lose an arm, they grow a new one. Amazing! It's just a little bud at first, but in a year or so, they've got a whole new arm.

Bailey: A year?

OLOTB: You don't suppose growing something new is easy, do you?

SWEET AND SOUR

On the boardwalk
just down from *The Clam Shell*
is a café that makes
the *best* cinnamon doughnuts—
fresh, buttery cakes,
sharp taste of cinnamon
tangled
in the white sugar
that sticks
to your lips,
melts
on your tongue.
I'd eat them every day
if I could.

It's usually busy
in the café,
but today's crazy—
people packed in,
filling every chair,
crowding the counter,

and everyone
talking
at once.
Nana Marie takes Kevin's hand,
tells me to grab on, too,
and we wind our way through,
a three-part snake
slithering
to the end of the queue.

A sundress-lady
pushes toward us,
hollers
so Nana Marie can hear
over the chaos.

      Good, she says, her voice cutting
through
the sugary sweet smell floating
in the room.

      You heard about the meeting.

Nana Marie hollers back:

      What meeting?

Turns out
word went 'round
that people should gather,
but it seems less like a meeting
and more like a fight,

everyone cranky,
full of complaints—
the town's birthday,
tourist traffic,
that *confounded man*
getting people riled up.

> *He's a nuisance—*

> *a thief—*

> *something*
> *must be done.*

Nana Marie decides
on take-out,
places our order
while bitterness swirls
through the café.

Someone else comes in,
light glaring
off the glass door,
blinding me.
A hush washes over the room
like a wave
moving from one side
to the other.
I squint at the figure
silhouetted in the door frame—

hard to see,
but I know
it's Jasper.

The last of the bickering
stops
when Jasper's river voice
flows.

> *It will come to pass*
> *that saving the life of one*
> *will save the souls*
> *of many.*

He scans the room,
nods in my direction,
turns away,
and leaves.

The room is quiet
until the bell jangles
as the door
latches.

> *What does he mean?*
> someone demands.

> *Heresy,* shouts a sundress-lady.
> *Blasphemy!*

Good heavens, Nana Marie says,
I hardly think so.

But murmurs rise,
a circle of discontent
spreading outward
from the sundress-lady
like rings on water
after a fish
leaps up,
twists around,
snaps its jaw shut
on a bug.

Nana Marie hands me the bag
of cinnamon doughnuts,
but there's a sour taste
in the air
that I'm afraid will ruin
everything.

SIDES

The box of *Archie* comics
sits between Kev and me
on the porch swing.
It's sizzling hot,
and here in the late afternoon shade
with a breeze from the sea
we're still sweating.
I'm about to get up,
go inside for lemonade,
when a man and a woman
walk up the path.
They stand at the porch steps,
ask for Nana Marie,
so Kevin zips inside
to get her.

I recognize the visitors.
They were dancing on the grass
at the party.
I wonder
if they were at the café yesterday,

forgetting the fun they had
and fighting
instead.

Nana Marie comes out
to talk with them.
Through the open window
a clatter of LEGO pieces
tells me Kevin
is staying inside.
I push with my toes,
set the swing moving,
listen
while I pretend to read
about Archie and Betty.

The visitors hand Nana Marie
a clipboard,
ask her to sign a petition
for a bylaw
against mobile
food
vendors.

*To maintain the character
of our town*, says the woman.

Quality control, says the man. *And safety
for pedestrians.*

Hogwash, says Nana Marie. *You want a bylaw
against Jasper.*

My toes dig into the floorboards.
The swing
stops.

Well, says the woman, *I suppose
it would affect Mr. Angelopoulos.*

I never mind about pretending
not to listen.

What's a bylaw? I ask.

Nana Marie says, *A law
just for our town.*

*So…no ice cream carts
in Felicity Bay?*

It's for the best, says the man,
flapping the front of his shirt
to cool himself.

But it's just ice cream, I say.
It's just Jasper.

Hush, Chickadee.

Nana Marie glances
at the clipboard.

Don't sign it, Nana Marie!

I try to snatch it
from her hands,
but she lifts it
out of my reach.
Her expression is a mixture
of anger
and…something.

Don't you worry, she says
handing the clipboard back to the woman.
*I've no intention of signing such
nonsense.*

The woman scowls,
shoves the clipboard
into her bag.

Given your history, she says,
*I'd have thought you'd be glad
to see him go.*

The man and the woman
who danced on the lawn
say nothing more
as they leave,

but the look on their faces
says the battle
is on.

If I were Jasper,
I'd be glad
to have Nana Marie on my side.
But I kind of hate
that there are sides.

HISTORY

When the petition people
are out of sight,
I sink back
onto the swing.
Nana Marie sits beside me,
pulls the box of comics
onto her lap.
She picks up the one on top,
chuckles
at the cover.

    That Reggie, she says. *What a character.*

This is no time
for changing
the subject.

    Why is everyone so upset?
    Why can't people
    just leave Jasper alone?

Nana Marie sighs,
drops the comic
back onto the pile.

History, Chickadee.
History.

What history?
Please—I want to understand.

It's a hard story
for me to tell.

She picks up the comic again.
I don't want to hear
about Reggie.
I'm about to protest,
but then Nana Marie takes the comic
by the spine,
uses it for a fan,
leans back in the porch swing,
and starts her story.

At church one Sunday—
this was three years ago—
Jasper stood up to say the benediction
but prophesied instead.
I'll never forget his words:

'It will come to pass
that adversity
and loss
will make their home
among us.'

You can imagine
it caused quite a stir.

What did it mean? I ask.

That trouble was coming.
And he was right.
That night at sunset
Harold went for a swim
like he did every day.

Nana Marie hesitates,
swallows hard.

He never came back.

Nana Marie stops talking,
stops fanning,
stares out toward the beach
as if she's still hoping Harold
will walk out of the sea
and come home.

Finally, she looks back at me.

I say, *Mom told me*
about Grandpa Harold.
I knew he drowned.
That's why you say
No Swimming Alone,
isn't it?

She nods,
hands me a comic book
from the box,
and the two of us wave our fans
as she continues.

Next morning, she says, *Monday—a fire*
destroyed the board shop.

Board shop?

Wake boards,
paddle boards,
a few surf boards.
All claimed
by the flames,
as if God or fate or something
didn't want people
out on the water.

She takes a slow breath
in
and out,
as if she's gathering strength
before carrying on.

Tuesday, the storm came.
I never saw such turmoil
on the sea—
dark water snarling at us
and grabbing whatever it could
in the white claws
of its waves.
Boats and docks damaged
and swamped
one after the other.
It went on all day,
until the stroke of midnight.
Rain and storms still come
on Tuesdays—
reminding us every week
that the sea
is no place to be.

But Daniel and I swim
all the time.
Nothing bad has happened.
Maybe a storm
is just a storm.

You're right, Chickadee. It is.
If I didn't believe that,
I'd have never let you go into
the water.
But for those of us who were there,
those of us who heard the prophecy—
well, fear makes people hold tight to things,
whether it makes sense
or not.

So people hate Jasper
because they're afraid?

Nana Marie purses her lips
the way she does when she's thinking.

Do you know what a benediction is?

I shake my head.

It's a blessing.
When Jasper opened his mouth to speak
at the end of church that day,
we were expecting a blessing.
The prophecy sounded like
a curse,
and in the days that followed,
sometimes it really did feel
like we'd been cursed.

A lot of people—me included—merged Jasper
and the prophecy
and the angry sea
into a single entity,
and we labeled it
Evil.

She's quiet, then—
rocking
and fanning
but not
talking.

That's a terrible story, I say.

Are you sorry you asked
to hear it?

No, but—
I nod toward the comic
in my hand—
Reggie doesn't seem so bad now,
does he?

Nana Marie laughs,
and it sounds
the way a cool breeze feels
on a scorching day.

BOXES

Next day Daniel and I
stop at the market
for root beer candy,
see Jasper coming out
with empty boxes—
big ones,
the kind you might use
for packing.

> *You're not leaving, are you?*
> *They won't get their dumb old bylaw—*
> *I know it! Nana Marie*
> *won't let that happen.*

Jasper smiles.
How can a person look sad
even though
he's smiling?
Like rain
from a clear blue sky.

Why would I stay? he says. *They think
I'm a fraud. They think
I stole the chalice.*

I tell him we'll search for it,
find the chalice,
prove he didn't do it.
Jasper piles the boxes
on the boardwalk—
a precarious tower
anyone could topple
if they weren't careful.

It's not about proof.

Sure, it is, I say. *Innocent
until proven guilty.*

*The prophecies, Bailey—
they're about faith,
not proof.*

But they're coming true!

I say it
without thinking
but I realize
they *are* coming true—
or at least
halfway.

A stranger
came from the sea.
A treasure
was lost.
I just need to know
how to make the other halves
come true,
but something tells me
that if Jasper goes,
it's all over.

> *I need them*
> *to come true.*

> *You'd be surprised*
> *what a little faith can do.*

Daniel has a coughing fit then,
and for a minute
I forget about faith,
prophecies,
and empty boxes.

> *You all right?* Jasper asks
when the fit
is finally over.

I should've been the one to ask—
he's *my* friend,

but knowing his lungs
don't work right
takes the words from my mouth
before I can say them.

> *I'm okay,* Daniel says.
> *Why do you say those things*
> *anyway? The prophecies, I mean.*

> Jasper says, *I don't know*
> *if those words were from me,*
> *or from God. I only know*
> *I needed to say them.*

> *They make people mad,* says Daniel.
> *Can't you take them back?*
> *Promise to stop?*

> *What good is truth*
> *if you bury it?*

I guess truth
is like treasure—
no good to anyone
if it's hidden,
tucked away in a box,
lost.

> *But,* says Jasper, *if people*
> *don't want to hear,*

maybe it's time to move on—
shake the dust
from my sandals, as they say,
and go.

He starts walking,
balancing the boxes
he'll fill with his things,
seal with tape,
load on a truck
that goes far away.

You can't leave! I say.

Leave
like Dad stomping out
after a fight,
like a friend moving away
with her mom,
people splitting apart
and leaving,
always leaving.

I have to make Jasper stop—
stop walking,
stop leaving,
stop giving up
on Felicity Bay.

If you go,
you won't see
how it all works out—
the prophecies
and the petition
and everything.

He looks back.

Doesn't matter, he says.
It was never
about
me.

UPSIDE DOWN

We watch the sunset
turn the sea tangerine
and gold.

> *I bet it's even better
> upside down,* says Nana Marie.

Then her hands
are down, her feet
are up—
a perfect handstand
on the beach.
Kevin kicks up his legs,
ends up facing the wrong way,
turns a half-circle on his hands
so he can see
the sea.
He laughs.

> *It's the same!* he says.

I try a handstand,
kick too hard,
land on my back
in the sand.
I try a few more times
then give up
and watch the sunset
bent over,
looking through my legs.
It really is the same—
sky reflected on water,
beautiful upside down
and right-side up.

We gather bits of driftwood,
make a campfire,
lean back against logs, and listen
to flames crackling
and waves shushing
on the beach.

> *There's a bag of marshmallows
> in the pantry*, says Nana Marie.

Kevin dashes off
to get them,
and I have Nana Marie
to myself.
Mom and Dad will be here
in a couple days,

and I've been trying to imagine
the difference marriage camp
might make.
I poke at the fire,
remember the photograph—
my parents smiling
by another campfire.

> *Is it hard*
> *to stay married?*

Nana Marie laughs,
but I didn't mean
to be funny.

> *I suppose it depends,* she says.

> *On what?*

> *On a lot of things.*
> *Everyone's different.*
> *For me, it would help*
> *if my husbands*
> *didn't keep dying.*

I'm not sure
if that's a joke,
but Nana Marie is quiet
for a moment, so I know
it wasn't.

Her first husband
was my real grandpa—
Mom's father.
He died when I was two.
I don't remember him.
Then there was Harold.
I wish I'd had a chance
to get to know him
like I'm getting to know
Nana Marie. I bet
they were quite a pair.

I ask if Harold
was very much like my grandpa.
Nana Marie shakes her head.

Like day and night, those two.

She looks at the view,
the last bits of color draining
from the scene.

Like air and water,
sky and sea. But you know,
in the right light,
they weren't so very different.

You mean how they looked?

No, she says.
How I loved them.

Do Mom and Dad
love each other
as much as Nana Marie
loved Harold
or my grandpa?
From the way they look
in their wedding pictures
and the way they used to dance
around the kitchen,
I know they were that much in love
once.
But now?

What happens when parents stop
being in love? What happens
to the kids?

My friend just lives with her mom now, I say.
I don't even know
if her dad loves her anymore.
Do you think...I mean,
what's going to happen if...

Nana Marie puts her arm
around my shoulders,
pulls me closer,
kisses my hair.

Parents never stop loving their kids.
Maybe you stop living together.
Maybe you don't even talk much,
but they don't stop loving you.
Not ever.

I can't imagine Dad
not living with us,
or Mom
not being there.
How do they decide
who goes?
What if it's me
that has to choose?

The cottage door bangs,
and a minute later
Kevin's back
with marshmallows but no
toasting forks.
We scrounge for sticks,
then cook
over the coals—
sweet
messy
goodness.

Later, we wash our hands
in the ocean.

It seems like a perfect night,
except for the thought
that slides into my head,
drifts down,
ties my stomach
in a sticky knot:

Is my life about to turn
upside down?

SECRET SPOTS

The new rungs
fastened to the tree
hold fast
as I climb up.

> *Check it out,* Daniel says
> once we're both
> in the tree house.

He lifts a loose floorboard.
I peer into the gap,
find our playing cards,
Daniel's binoculars,
a flashlight,
all hiding
in a secret compartment.
Coolest
thing
ever.

> *Rigged it up last night.*
> *Now we need a shelf—*

a decoy storage spot
so people won't think to look
in the floor.

Daniel chooses a piece of wood
already cut
from one of Jasper's fence boards.
I hold it in place
while he hammers.
The noise echoes
in my head,
vibrations rattle
my arms.
He reaches for another nail.

My dad's taking me
to the hardware store tomorrow, he says.
Gonna rig up a pulley system
so we don't have to stuff everything
in our pockets.

Tomorrow…

He starts banging
on the nail.

My parents arrive tomorrow.

Daniel stops hammering.

*Does that mean you and Kevin
are going home?*

*Not yet. We're all staying
another week.*

*Good. We still need to find
the treasure.*

One treasure lost,
a greater one found—
we've no clue
where the chalice might be,
but Daniel still thinks
the *greater* treasure,
the one that will be found,
could be at the church.
I really don't think
we should dig up the churchyard,
but we *have* to find it,
have to prove Jasper
is for real,
prove the prophecies
are for real.
And then maybe,
Jasper will stay.

As soon as the shelf
is secure,
we nab Levi and Kevin
to help us hunt.

When I lost my iPod, Levi says,
turned out it was in my room
all along.

Kevin asks if Levi thinks the treasure
is in his bedroom.

No, Levi says—
and he doesn't laugh
at Kevin's idea—
  it's just that sometimes
  what you're looking for
  is right there in plain sight.

We decide to look *in*
the church,
hoping the greater treasure
will be right there in view,
like Levi's iPod.

The church is locked,
but a window in the basement
is open.
Kevin is smallest
and bendiest,
so he shimmies inside,
scoots across the room,
opens
the basement door.

My stomach shimmies, too,
but the hope of treasure
and proof
and fixing things for Jasper
is too much
to resist.
I follow everyone inside,
up the stairs,
into the sanctuary—
stained glass,
silent organ,
empty pews.

      Maybe the greater treasure, says Daniel,
      is a bigger chalice.
      A fancier one.

We spread out,
look around,
but don't see a chalice
or anything else
that seems like treasure.

Something rattles
by the big wood doors.
I freeze,
then all at once
the four of us
hear the jingle
of keys. Someone
is coming.

Oh-man-we're-in-for-it
fills my bones,
shifts my feet
into slow motion.
Even if we had time
to run for the basement,
there's no way
I could do it.

We slide under pews,
lie on our bellies
on the hardwood,
try
not
to breathe.

The door opens,
sunlight slices
through the room
like a spotlight.
I see sandals
and socks.
The feet pause,
door closes,
room dims.
I glance at Kevin—
wild eyes,
lips pinched together
like he's trying to hold in noises
that want to burst out.

I lift a finger
to my mouth.
Kevin dips his head
and stays quiet.

S-l-o-w-l-y
I lean to one side
for a better look.
It's Reverend Davidson.
He walks up the aisle
past Daniel,
Levi,
Kevin,
me,
steps up to the pulpit,
and I wonder
if he's going to practice his sermon
with four kids
hiding
under the pews,
but he reaches out,
takes a book from the pulpit,
and leaves
the way he came in.
I finally
breathe.

No one moves
until the lock
clicks,

then we slither
from our hiding spots,
take off
down the stairs,
hands pressed over mouths,
smothering
our laughter.

～

*Bailey: You are going to change everything, aren't you?
Like Jasper said. Even if he leaves?*

OLOTB: Come with me.

Bailey: Where? Can you even move?

OLOTB: I'd like to go for a swim.

*Bailey: I'm not allowed to go in the water alone. Nana
Marie's rule.*

OLOTB: I'll be with you.

Bailey: But…are you real? Really real?

OLOTB: Take my hand.

*Bailey: How am I supposed to swim holding hands? I
need both arms.*

OLOTB: …

Bailey: Okay, I'll try. But not too deep!

*OLOTB: You can't call it swimming if your feet are on
solid ground.*

Bailey: Don't let go.

OLOTB: I never do.

～

A LITTLE FAITH

Daniel's mom stands
behind an easel
on their porch,
paintbrush in hand,
staring
at the sea.
She sends us inside
for a snack.

In the kitchen
Levi hands Daniel a pill bottle
with his banana bread.

> *Hang on,* Daniel says.
> *I need to recharge*
> *my camera battery.*

He disappears
into the other room.
Levi and I hear his coughing
out here.

Doesn't that scare you,
I ask. *It sounds*
awful.

Guess I'm used to it, Levi says,
but yeah,
it still scares me
when he can't breathe.

Daniel's harsh cough
goes on
and
on.
His mom steps inside,
listens,
shakes her head.

It's getting worse, she says to Levi.

Yeah, he says.

He'll be okay, though,
right? I say.

His mom smiles at me—
the don't-worry-sweetie kind of smile
that moms do.

Yes, she says. *He will.*

But how do you know?

Just have to have faith
sometimes.

That afternoon,
her words float back to me
when I'm lying on my bunk
trying to read
but thinking
instead.
Have faith, she said.
Jasper said I'd be surprised
what a little faith
can do.
I'm trying to have faith,
trying to believe everything
will be okay.
But what if things *don't* work out?
What if Jasper leaves,
Daniel can't breathe,
my parents aren't in love?
What if my family falls apart,
and I have to choose one parent
and not
the other?
Then what good
is faith?

The turquoise sea glass
from Daniel
still sits on my windowsill.
I climb down from my bunk,
pluck it from the ledge,
rub it
with my thumb.
It whispers to me
of mermaids,
prophecies,
hope—
and I know
I can't give up.

My parents will be here
tomorrow,
and they simply *have* to
be changed.
Our Lady of the Bay
came to help—
everything must be fixed by now,
or at least
getting there.
So maybe,
instead of worrying,
I should be
believing,
getting ready to celebrate
my parents still loving each other,
and marriage camp
working.

How better to celebrate
than with cake?

I tuck the sea glass
in my shorts pocket,
find Nana Marie outside
picking blackberries.
I tell her my plan.
Her brows pull together
and the corners of her mouth
turn down.

> *I don't know, Chickadee.*

> *It's a step of faith,* I say.
> *Please?*

She looks hard at me,
then sighs.

> *Well,* she says, *I suppose*
> *I can't argue*
> *with that.*

She brings the berry bucket inside,
riffles through the recipe box,
pulls out a card.

> *Sugar can't fix everything,* she says
> as she hands over the recipe.

I know, I say,
but miracles can.

*Oh, Bailey. I'm just not sure
you should get your hopes up.*

Isn't *up*
where hopes
are supposed to be?

Nana Marie goes back
to her berry picking, and I
measure,
mix,
bake,
breathe in that sugary sweet smell.
While it cools
I make frosting—white
and pink,
like the cake
in Mom and Dad's wedding photos.
I spread on the white,
use the pink
to write *Happy Marriage*
instead of birthday
or anniversary,
draw a big
pink
heart
that usually stands for love,

but today
stands for a little
faith.

Now if only the miracle
prophecy
change-everything part
works out.

I wonder
if I should do more,
if it would still be faith
if I helped things along.
Maybe a romantic dinner for Mom and Dad
when they arrive—
but no...I tried that before.
I tried
everything.
Or at least
almost everything.

I get permission from Nana Marie
to use her computer,
search for their song—
the one they told me
they danced to
at their wedding,
the one Mom used to sing
to Kev and me
when we were little,

the one that used to play so often
from the speakers
in our family room.
I listen to a few wrong ones
before finding the right one,
the one that sounds
like a grandfather—
rough voice
but friendly
and somehow
perfect
as he sings
about a wonderful
world.
I download it,
then head outside
to search
for wildflowers.

COLD AND GRAY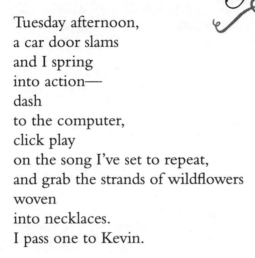

Tuesday afternoon,
a car door slams
and I spring
into action—
dash
to the computer,
click play
on the song I've set to repeat,
and grab the strands of wildflowers
woven
into necklaces.
I pass one to Kevin.

You can put Mom's on her, I tell him.
I'll do Dad's.

Last night I heard Nana Marie
talking on the phone
with Mom.

You sound more...relaxed, Nana Marie said.

A pause, then:

So you've worked something out?

The call ended
after that, so I think Mom was saving
the worked-something-out news
for today.
Working things out
is good!
Energy bubbles inside me,
makes me antsy—
can't wait
to see them,
can't wait
for still-in-love dancing,
hugging,
laughing,
staying
together.
Can't wait
for the miracle
to finally be seen.

Kevin and I scramble
to our places
just as
knock knock knock
and the door opens.
Mom
lets herself in,
shirt rain-speckled,

small gray suitcase
drops
from her hand
and she bends down,
opens her arms
as Kevin launches himself at her.
After a few seconds
they untangle
and Kevin holds out the garland
of flowers.
Mom ducks her head
so he can put it on her.

A lei! she says. *It's beautiful!*

Bailey made it, says Kevin. *I tried
to help, but mine kept breaking.*

The wonderful-world song
begins again.
Mom hugs me
hard
then moves her suitcase
so she can close
the door.
Poor Dad, stuck unloading the car
in the rain. I glance
out the front window,
can't see him,
look again.

Where's Dad? I say,
fingering the lei
I'm waiting
to put 'round his neck.

Mom glances over my shoulder
to where Nana Marie
leans in the doorway
of the kitchen,
clutching
a dishtowel.
Then Mom looks back at me,
reaches out a hand
to pull Kevin closer,
draws us in,
and in that moment
she deflates
as if someone
pulled a plug—
all her joy and energy
escaping,
disappearing
into the air.

He's not coming? says Kevin.

Mom shakes her head.

He'll meet us back home.

Why back home? I say.
Why not here?

She doesn't answer,
but I know.
My throat closes up,
stomach clenches.
I push away from her,
plunk the wildflower lei
on the desk,
stop
the music.

In the silence,
Nana Marie serves iced tea—
tall glasses on a white tray
as if we were company.
We don't drink it,
just hold the glasses
and examine ice cubes.

Mom and Nana Marie sit
on the ocean-blue couch,
one on each end,
legs crossed,
faces turned away.
There's a hard edge in the air
that reminds me of the sea
when it's cold
and gray,
waves smashing the shore
like doors slamming.

Kevin disappears.
Every time I think
of something to say,
the words dissolve
on my tongue.
Finally I take my glass
and slink
to the kitchen.
Maybe they'll talk
if I disappear, too.

A clink of ice.

Mom clearing her throat.

I listen hard
for her voice.

      We're separating, she says.

The words
wrap around my chest,
squeeze hard,
pressure
as if I were sitting
on the ocean floor,
water pushing in
and no
air.

For good? Nana Marie asks.

For a while.

I don't know how long
a while is,
but I'm pretty sure
it's much
too
long.

*I think we've got the details
worked out—where he'll stay,
when he'll see the kids.*

My eyes sting.
The ocean's still pressing in,
but I'm at the fridge,
door open,
butter knife in hand,
everything blurry
through my tears.
My hand reaches in,
scrapes off
pink words,
pink heart,
leaving an ugly glob
of icing and crumbs
smeared
on the shelf.

Kevin's not in our room,
but I wish he was,
because alone
is too lonely right now.
I shut the door
and then…
a small sound.

I bend down,
peer
under the bunk beds.
A bundle of sheets
or maybe
a boy
in a sheet
under the bed.
I pull my quilt
from the top bunk,
spread it on the floor,
lie down and listen
to the ebb and flow
of his breath.

Did they try?
Four weeks and now
Mom is here
and Dad
isn't.
It's like they failed
marriage camp.

How do you fail camp?
Maybe it's their fault
there was no miracle,
their fault
nothing changed.
Maybe it was stupid
to wish for miracles,
stupid
to hope that a mermaid
could do God-work,
stupid
to believe
magical things can happen.

Or…

 maybe…

a breeze lifts the curtains,
lets in a breath
of rain-soaked air

…maybe *Our Lady of the Bay*
is still waiting
for the right moment.

FLOOD

Mom and Nana Marie argue
in the living room.
Their words drift up the stairs
to my room
like smoke rising
from a wildfire.

You've no idea
how upset she must be,
says Nana Marie.

Yes, I do, Mom says.
But it's not really your concern.

Yes, it is. Bailey—

She'll adjust,
given some time.

I don't know, Nana Marie says.
I'm worried about her.
Kevin, too. He—

You think I'm not worried?
I'm worried sick! But I think I know my children
better than you do.

I don't want to hear
any more,
but their voices
grow louder,
a thunder storm
closing in.

Only because you kept them from me
all these years.

Can you blame me?
You're hardly a good influence.

And yet you seem to think
you turned out fine.

Kevin hides
in our closet,
door closed,
Archie comic and flashlight
to distract him.
I grab Mom and Dad's photo
from the dresser,
shove it in my pocket,
then sneak out
and run through the downpour
to the tree house.

The roof leaks
in three spots,
but I'm wet anyway—
tears and rain—
so it doesn't matter.

How can they do this
to us? And Kevin—
Don't they know how much
he hates
this kind of storm,
how he can't sleep,
how he gets so
scared?

I pull out the picture,
scowl
at their happy faces.
I can't believe
they're splitting up.
This is all
SO
DUMB.

My fingers grasp
the loose floorboard.
I lift one end,
drop the picture
in our secret spot,
slam it closed.

After a while I remember
I'm not like Kevin,
don't want to be
alone.
I climb down,
go around the front
of Daniel's house,
knock
on the door.
No one's home,
and rain's coming down,
strange wind howling
through the trees.

Nana Marie slumps on the porch swing,
a hard look on her face
but sorrow
in the lines
around her eyes.

> *Tide's going to be*
> *mighty high tonight*, she says.

It's high already, I think,
like a soup bowl filled
to the brim,
ready to slosh
over the edge.

Nana Marie looks straight at me
as if she just noticed
I was there.

Go on in and dry off, she says.

She goes back to watching the tide
creep in.

I leave my flip flops on the porch,
walk through the kitchen,
wet footprints
trailing behind me.
The bathroom door is closed.
I *tap tap tap,*
and Mom's voice says,

I'm in the tub.

Drips fall from my rain-soaked hair,
splatting on the floor,
filling the hallway,
the whole cottage,
flooding,
or at least
needing a good mop.

I crack open Nana Marie's bedroom door
and slip inside.

We're not allowed in here,
but right now
I don't even care.
I cross over to Nana Marie's bathroom
for a towel,
grab a striped one
from the rack,
raise it to my hair,
gasp.

I swear,
for a moment
my heart
stops.

There on the vanity
beside Nana Marie's sink
is a beautiful
silver
cup.

A chalice.

The chalice.

I back out,
heart pounding,
close the door
carefully,
quietly,

hide the towel in my room
and creep
into bed.
Even though
I'm on the top bunk,
I'm caught in a rip tide,
a rush of questions
pulling me away,
pulling me
under.

I lie there a long time
trying
not to drown,
trying
to understand.

GONE

Sea grass still wet
from yesterday's rain
flings drops
onto my legs
as I push through
to the beach.
Daniel won't be finished
his treatments yet,
but I need to think before I see him
anyway.

If I tell him Nana Marie
is a thief,
will he still
be my friend?
Will he say
I have to turn her in?
Because I can't do that,
can't tell the truth—
she's my nana.
I only just got to know her,
not ready
to give her up.

What if the police
take her away?
She said Reverend Davidson
wouldn't call the cops,
but what if he does?

I need some time
to sort things out,
need some time
with *Our Lady of the Bay.*
Jasper said she would change
everything—
I just didn't know
so much *everything*
would need changing.

I'm almost there.
The scattered driftwood
glows golden
in the morning sun.
I can't see her.
I scan the beach again.
Her kelp hair
must've come off
in the storm.
I search
for replacement kelp,
find a piece that will do
for now,
grab it,
and look up.

I walked right past
the spot.

I retrace my steps.
This is the place—
I'm sure of it,
but she's not here.

I stare at the logs—
different ones,
new ones—
and I remember
the strange wind,
the fierce storm.

I turn slowly to glare
at the sea.

> *You took her back*, I say.
> *You took*
> *the mermaid.*

No wonder
everything's
going
wrong.

My feet fly
over the sand.

I arrive at Daniel's
breathing hard,
can barely talk
when Levi opens the door.

> *I need*
> *to see*
> *Daniel.*

Levi says nothing,
opens the door wider
so I can come in.
He pours a glass of water,
hands it to me.
I gulp some down.

> *Daniel's not here,* Levi says.

> *He's done his treatments*
> *already?*
> *That was fast.*

Levi shakes his head.

> *Last night my parents*
> *took him to the hospital.*
> *Lung infection—*
> *a bad one.*

I lower my glass
to the counter
because it feels
like it might slip from my hand,
smash
on the kitchen floor.

He'll be okay, right?

Sure, of course, Levi says,
but his face does a lousy job
of looking sure.
He's had infections before.

I nod,
force my mouth
to smile,
pretend I'm not worried,
and tell Levi
I have to go.

BEEP...BEEP...

Daniel's at the hospital in Victoria
because there isn't one
on Arbutus Island.
Mom and I take the ferry
so I can visit him.

Mom drives down the ramp
onto the boat,
pulls the car up close
to the truck ahead of us,
shuts off the engine.
She settles back in her seat
to wait out the crossing.

Thanks for driving me, I say.

No problem, she says.
*I'm sure he'll appreciate
a visitor. Plus,
it gives us a chance
to talk.*

Mom glances at me.
The ship's whistle
blasts.

I'm going up front, I say,
and I get out of the car,
walk to the bow
to feel the wind and salt spray
on my face.

I stay there until the ferry
approaches the dock near Victoria,
then return to the car,
buckle up,
stare straight ahead.

The ferry bumps,
jostles,
stops,
and a few minutes later
we're driving up the ramp,
out of the terminal,
and into the city.

I know you must be upset, Mom says.

He'll be okay.

*Yes. I'm sure he will. But I meant
about Dad and me.*

He's moving out
for a while,
but it's not final, you know.
It just seems like the best option
for now.

Hmph.

What?

How can it be the best option?
It's not the best anything.

Your dad and I—we tried.
We really did.

You need to keep trying.

We will.
We are—separating for a while
is a way of trying.

It's a stupid way.

Mom sighs,
puts on the turn signal,
waits.

It's not ideal. But you and Kev
will adjust.

Kevin's probably going to sleep under the bed
for the rest of his life.

Kevin will take some time
to get used to things. But he'll be fine.

Mom moves the car forward,
turning left.

You don't know that! I say.

She didn't see him all wrapped up,
hiding
under the bunk.

You don't even care.

A car horn blares.
Mom slams on the brakes.
A minivan swerves
around us.
We're silent the rest of the way
to the hospital.

Mom helps me find Daniel's room.
I introduce her
to his parents,
and the three of them
go for coffee
so Daniel and I
can visit.

Daniel looks small—
was he always
so skinny?
A sour taste rises
at the back of my throat.
I swallow it down,
try to smile.

Beep.

Beep.

I think he's taking pictures
from his hospital bed,
but then the machine beside him
beeps again.

> *Antibiotics*, he says
> pointing to the bag of fluid
> dripping into his arm
> through a tube.

A nurse comes into the room,
fiddles with the machine,
and the beeping
stops.

Daniel lets me sit
on the side of his bed.

I don't tell him
about Nana Marie,
but I tell him everything else—
my parents separating
and the storm
carrying the mermaid
out to sea.

> *Now the prophecy*
> *will never come true,* I say.
> *A stranger from the sea*
> *will change everything.*

He says, *You know the mermaid*
wasn't real, right?

I'm not crazy.
I know
she was made of driftwood,
but something inside me
hangs on,
as if letting go,
admitting the truth,
will set me adrift,
a rowboat
pushed from the dock
without oars.
My throat tightens.

If she's not real, I say,
then the prophecies
aren't real,
Jasper
is a fake,
and nothing
will be changed.
If she's not real,
there's no
magic.

KEEPING SECRETS

Silence
fills the space
between Mom and Nana Marie.
It's worse
than the arguing.
Mom must think so, too,
because after lunch dishes
are done, Mom puts away
the last plate,
shuts the cupboard door
hard.

I'm going for a swim, she says.

I'm afraid if I stay
with Nana Marie,
she'll be able to tell
just by looking at me
that I went in her room,
saw the chalice,
know her secret,
so I say, *I'll go with you,*
and hurry to change.

We walk
to where the huge flat rocks
take the place of sand
and pebbles.
We wade in,
hold up our arms,
suck in our bellies,
as if that'll make the ocean
feel warmer.
The water's so clear,
sun cutting through
to the stone floor.
I step over a purple starfish
lounging
on the bottom.

A gull screeches overhead.
Mom and I look
at each other.

       Ready? Mom asks.

We both dive under,
come up with a gasp
and laughter.
After taking a few strokes,
diving under again,
coming up,
Mom says,

I'd forgotten
how refreshing this is.

I think of Nana Marie's story
about the water—
how people quit swimming
and quit being happy.
Mom and Nana Marie
aren't happy,
don't get along,
but I know
it's not about
the sea.

Why'd you stop coming here? I ask.
Why don't you like
Nana Marie?

Mom's smile fades.

I like her, she says, but
it's complicated.

I'm not dumb, you know.
Just because it's complicated
doesn't mean I won't get it.
Why is it all such a
big
stupid
secret?

Mom dunks
under the surface,
tips her head back
on the way up,
smoothes her hair.
She wipes the water
from her face.

> *Nana Marie and I*
> *had a falling out,* she says,
> as if that wasn't obvious.

> *No kidding,* I say,
and she frowns
at my attitude.

> *When I'm grown up,* I say,
> *I'll still want to see you.*
> *Even if we have a fight,*
> *no matter what*
> *it's about,*
> *I'll still talk to you.*

> *Oh, Bailey.*

She wipes her face again,
and I'm not sure
if it's ocean
or tears.

Your Nana Marie married Harold
very soon after your grandfather
died—too soon,
like she'd already
forgotten him.
It wasn't right.
It hurt me
deeply.

She loved Harold, I say,
but she loved Grandpa, too—
like air and water.

Mom's eyebrows pull together.

And anyway, I say,
ignoring her confusion,
it was a long time ago.

Mom sighs,
nods slowly.

I wasn't sure
I should leave you two
with her. She always was
a bit unusual.

I decide I'll never tell Mom
about the chalice,
because that's more than a bit
unusual,

and I want to be allowed
to come back someday.

We've had enough
of the cold,
squeeze water from our hair,
wrap ourselves
in towels.

> *Did you have fun here?*
> *Do you like Felicity Bay?*

> *It's great!* I say,
and a whoosh of guilt
runs through me.
I should tell her I missed her
in case I hurt her feelings,
but
I'm still mad at her,
still mad
at Dad,
still mad they're splitting up,
and still mad
about not knowing
Nana Marie.
I don't know what to say
about the Mom-and-Dad stuff,
> so I say, *All this time*
> *I've had a grandma*
> *and I never got to see her.*

Bailey—

She looks miserable,
squeezing her lips together hard
like she does when she's upset.
I hate it
when she's upset.
I make my voice as calm
as I can.

> *But at least I finally got to know her*
> *this summer.*

She nods,
smiles the kind of smile
that looks like it might
slip off her face
and blow away
in the breeze.

> *And you met a new friend,* she says.

She probably thinks
reminding me of Daniel
will make me happy,
and it does,
but it's a sad sort of happiness,
the kind that feels sharp
when it reaches
your heart.

Daniel should be here—
should be swimming with me,
should be healthy,
not hooked up
to beeping machines
in a hospital.

My eyes water,
and a secret fear
I didn't even know I had
spills out:

what if he
dies?

THE RIGHT THING

Sunday morning
I wake everyone up,
tell them
we're going to church.

> *What about pancakes?*
> says Nana Marie.

> *Pancakes might seem*
> *important,* I say,
sending signals
with my eyes,
hoping
Nana Marie realizes
I'm not talking about pancakes
at all.
> *But no matter why*
> *you want something,*
> *it's more important*
> *to do the right thing*
> *and go*
> *to*
> *church.*

My brain tries to beam
into Nana Marie's,
but she doesn't get
the message.

> *Well then,* she says,
> *cold cereal it is.*

She unstacks the bowls.

> *But I wanted pancakes,* Kevin says.

When we arrive at church,
the minister notices us
and smiles,
but not fast enough
to hide the hint of surprise
on his face.

> *Back so soon?* he says to Nana Marie.
> *It's nice to see you.*

Once we're sitting in a pew,
Kevin beside Mom,
me beside Nana Marie,
> I say, *You don't come here often,*
> *do you?*

> *I used to,* Nana Marie says.
> *Every Sunday,*
> *until Harold died.*

You didn't want to come
without Harold?

I didn't want to come
and have to see Jasper.

But he doesn't come now either.
And he misses Harold
too.

Nana Marie puts a finger to her lips,
nods toward the front
where Reverend Davidson
moves into place
behind the pulpit.

I whisper, *I bet Jasper*
would like someone to share
stories with. Stories
about Harold.

Nana Marie keeps looking
straight ahead.

He's leaving you know—
Jasper, I mean.
Leaving Felicity Bay.

I have to do something,
have to fix this.

Nana Marie might get upset
with me
for discovering her secret,
even though
it was an accident,
and she may not want me
to visit again,
and if I can't visit Nana Marie
I can't visit Daniel…

but

but

but

Jasper is innocent.

My voice is a bit shaky:
      What would Harold think now?

My eyes shift from Nana Marie
to the communion table
and back.
She stares at me,
and a deep line forms
between her eyebrows.

      The chalice, I whisper. *Jasper
      was Harold's friend.*

I look again
at the table—
at the empty spot
where the chalice should be.
Her gaze follows mine.
When she looks back at me,
her expression
makes me shrink
into the pew.
She stands up,
squishes past us,
marches to the back of the church,
and leaves.

The church service starts.
I can't pay attention—
forget to stand,
forget to sit,
don't hear a word
of the sermon.
Mom reaches past Kevin,
nudges me,
gives me a look
that says an earful,
but all I can think about
is Jasper,
and Nana Marie,
and what-have-I-done,
and not seeing Daniel.

Daniel.

Five days in the hospital now,
so I pray
for Daniel,
hope
there's a God up there
listening.

The service is over—
people filling the aisle,
everyone moving
to the heavy wooden doors
at the back,
and Nana Marie
clutching her big purse,
making her way
to the front,
a fish swimming
upstream.

She goes right up
where the minister stood
just a moment ago,
stops at the table,
reaches into her purse,
pulls out
the chalice,
and plunks it
next to the offering plates.

A GREATER TREASURE

Mom doesn't want help.
She shoos everyone out to the porch
while she fixes sandwiches.
Kevin runs down to the beach
to hunt for crabs,
which he's discovered
are even cooler
than bugs.
Nana Marie sits
on the porch swing
where she can keep an eye on him.
I slip off the porch
to follow Kevin,
but Nana Marie calls me back,
pats the seat beside her,
so I plod back,
sink onto the corner
of the swing.

Are you mad at me? I ask.

No, she says. *But I expect
you're angry with me.*

I don't know what to say.
I'm not angry, exactly.
More like a combo pack of
surprised-confused-disappointed.

> Finally I say, *I just don't understand*
> *how you could do that*
> *to Jasper,*
> *how you could let people go on believing*
> *he was guilty.*
> *He was your friend!*

Nana Marie nods.

> *He was. Yes.*
> *Maybe he will be again,*
> *if he'll forgive me.*

> *But you knew they were accusing him…*

She sighs,
and the last bit of liveliness
drains from her
like the world dimming
when clouds
overtake the sun.

> *I suppose part of me*
> *has always needed someone*
> *to blame*
> *for Harold being gone.*

Jasper, unfortunately,
was the most convenient.
It wasn't a big step from there
to letting others
think badly of him.

She looks at me
for a moment
before turning her gaze
back to where Kevin
paws around
in a tide pool.

And, she says,
there was also a part of me
that felt justified
in taking back the chalice.

Taking it back?

You have to understand
about the chalice.
I didn't take it
to spite Jasper. See,
Harold gave it to the church
as a thank you
when Jasper married us—
he was the minister back then.

Then…
the prophecies started,
Harold died,
and I quit going to church.

But you took me and Kevin, I say.

Yes, I did—
after three years away!
It's a wonder Reverend Davidson
didn't keel over
from the shock.

She chuckles,
then grows serious again.

When I saw the chalice again
after all that time,
my feelings about Harold
came rushing back—
how happy he looked
on our wedding day,
how much I loved him,
how very much
I miss him…

So you took it?

I still can't believe
Nana Marie is a thief.

A memory
wiggles its way
into my mind—
weeks ago,
a spoon
of significance
from Marina Grill.

Oh.

But no one was mad at anyone
over that.
No one was being chased
out of town.

>   *Don't you see?* she says.
>   *It's a cup of significance.*
>   *A reminder of Harold,*
>   *of our wedding,*
>   *of family.*
>   *I don't have family anymore—*
>   *not really.*

Sadness is draped
all over her,
so I stop wondering
if she's angry
or if I am,
and I scooch closer to her
on the swing.

You've got us, I say. *Me and Kev.*

She smiles a little,
pats my hand.

> *Thank you, Chickadee,*
> *but I suspect this visit*
> *is a one-off—*
> *just a convenience*
> *for your parents.*
> *Don't get me wrong—*
> *it's been delightful*
> *having you here with me.*
> *But time passes. Things*
> *change.*

> *Maybe you could visit us,*
> I say. *Come for Christmas dinner,*
> *get a spoon*
> *for your collection.*

She laughs,
gives the swing a push,
like she's giving herself time
to think.

> *I don't expect*
> *that would work out,* she says
> after a few back-and-forths.

I tell her I know
about the falling out
between her and Mom.

> *Your mother never really forgave me*
> *for managing to love*
> *someone else.*

> *That's crazy,* I say.
> *There can never be*
> *too much love.*

> *You'd like to think*
> *that was true,*
> *but when Harold and I got married,*
> *your mother refused*
> *to come to the wedding.*
> *I suppose I never forgave her*
> *for that.*

I upset my mom sometimes,
do something dumb
that makes her mad,
but I can't imagine her
being angry with me
forever.

> *But Nana Marie,* I say,
> *you're her mom. And you said*
> *parents don't stop loving*
> *their kids.*

She sucks in a breath,
puts a hand
over her mouth.
Her voice
is a whisper.

Oh, Bailey.

Her hand drifts down
to her lap.

I haven't stopped loving her.
But you're right, Chickadee. I know,
you're right.
We don't stop being family
just because
things change.

And suddenly
I'm thinking
of Mom and Dad and Kevin and me—
I know one thing
for certain:
we don't stop being family
if things change.
We don't stop being family
ever.

The cottage door bangs.
Mom strides over,
apron flapping,
face wet
with tears.

> *All these years*, she says
> to Nana Marie, *I never looked at it
> from your side. I never thought
> how alone you were
> after Harold died.*

Nana Marie glances away from Mom,
twisting
to look behind her.
I look, too.
The kitchen window
is wide open—
Mom must've heard
everything.

> *Well,* says Nana Marie,
> settling back in her seat,
> *I don't suppose I understood
> your side of things
> either.*

> *What you said earlier—
> despite everything,
> we're still…*

Family, says Nana Marie,
and Mom nods.

Neither of them
makes a move.
I feel stuck in the middle,
a stubborn grown-up
on each side of me,
waiting
for who knows what.

> *Well,* I say,
> *maybe we should start*
> *acting like it.*

> *Bailey!*

Mom hates it
when I have attitude.
Now, though, she laughs.

Nana Marie gets up,
swing rocking behind her,
and for the first time
since Mom got here,
they hug each other.

Kevin rushes up the path,
hands cupped.

Look at this huge one
I caught!

He thrusts his cupped hands
toward me,
lifts the fingers of one hand
like a lid:
a seaweed-green crab
skitters
across his palm,
pincers flailing.

He needs to go back
to the beach, Mom says,
one arm still wrapped
around Nana Marie.
Lunch is ready.

Kevin dashes through sea grass,
clambers
over driftwood,
dumps the crab in a tide pool
before running back
to join us.
We file
into the cottage.

So, says Mom, *tell me*
about the chalice.

Nana Marie chuckles,
ruffles Kevin's hair,
says she doesn't need
any chalice
because she's got something
much greater.

One prophecy
comes true:
one treasure will be lost
and a greater one
found.

CHANGE

Jasper's ice cream cart
is parked on the walkway
by the pier,
all shined up,
a *For Sale* sign dangling
from the handle bars.

News about Nana Marie
and the chalice
spread through town
as if the sea breeze
carried her confession—
blew it
through open windows
to everyone's ears.
I wonder if they're gossiping
about Nana Marie now
instead
of Jasper.
I wonder if it matters
she did it for love.

I rest my elbows
on the wooden railing
of the pier,
look out
over the water,
feel a stone
settle in my stomach.
Two more days—
that's all I've got
before I have to pack up,
leave Nana Marie's,
go home
to where Dad
isn't.

Far below on the beach
something's washed up,
half in the water,
half out.
I squint against the sun,
lean forward,
see it move.

Did it move?

I watch again,
wait,
squint harder,
lean further.
Yes!

I run to the canteen
on the pier,
holler at the guy
working inside.

He digs around
and finally comes out
with binoculars.

> *Looks like a dolphin,*
> he says.

> *We've got to help it!*

> *Don't worry*, the guy says.
> *Tide's coming in.*

That can't be right.
If it's coming *in,*
how did the dolphin
get stuck?
How did the beach
get wet?

> *Nuh-uh*, I say.

It's going out,
and that dolphin
is in trouble.

I haven't seen a dolphin
since the day Kev and I
first came
to the island.
I didn't even know Nana Marie
back then,
or Daniel,
or Jasper,
or even Agnes
or the flowery-sundress ladies.
I was a stranger
arriving on the ferry.

I was a stranger
coming
across
the sea.

My heart speeds up,
hand slaps
over my mouth.
Why didn't I see it before?

I'm the stranger
from the sea.

Me.

And I have to change
everything.

I don't know how
to fix things,
don't know how
to make a difference.
All I know
is I'm starting
with the dolphin.

THE NEED TO BREATHE

I run from the pier,
down the path,
smack hard
into Jasper.

A dolphin, I say,
on the beach.

I see it, Jasper says.
Get help—and a bucket.

I sprint
to the closest house,
bang
bang
bang
on the door
till it opens.
Even though the lady
wears matching blue shorts
and shirt,
I know
she's a sundress-lady.

I tell her there's a dolphin
beached
in the bay,
       say, *Jasper needs a bucket.*

       Jasper? she says,
       face pinching up
       like she's smelling
       rotten seaweed.

My hands curl
into fists.
I yell at her:
       I don't care
       what you think of his prophecies—
       when someone needs help,
       you help!

She stands there
staring at me
out of her pinched-up face,
so I take off,
bang on the next door
and the next.
I get to Daniel's house,
bang
bang
bang.
Levi will help, I know it,
and he does—

grabs a tarp Daniel bought
for the leaky tree house
while I go next door
to get Mom
and Nana Marie.

Nana Marie picks up
the phone.

> *No one's better*
> *at spreading the word*
> *than Agnes,* she says,
> and she punches in
> the number.

I race for the beach,
leap
over driftwood,
hoping people will come
to help.

They do.

Before long Nana Marie
and Mom
and the sundress-lady
are scooping up seawater
with yogurt containers,
splashing it
over the dolphin.

That's the best I could find,
the sundress–lady says,
nodding
at the containers.

That's okay, I say.
They're fine!

Jasper and Levi are on their knees
beside the dolphin
looking like they're praying,
but instead
they're scraping sand away,
making a shallow ditch,
working hard and fast.
The tide's even further out now,
and the dolphin's as stuck
as ever.
I suddenly feel
helpless,
don't know
what else to do.

I'm not sure
if the dolphin's friendly
or dangerous,
but I'll bet he's scared.
I crouch down,
put my hand
on his rubbery skin,

wonder if it's hard
for him to breathe
out here on the sand,
no water
to take his weight.

I think of Daniel—
how hard it is
sometimes
for him to breathe—
and I need to get this dolphin
back to the sea,
because so much depends
on breath.

WALKING INTO THE SEA

I look up—
Agnes,
Reverend Davidson,
the petition lady,
people I don't even recognize,
all streaming
toward us.

      Bailey, says Jasper, *dig.*

I pull sand away,
scooping,
clawing,
creating a tunnel
beneath the dolphin.
Then the tarp's peeking through
from the other side
and I'm flinging sand,
tugging
at the tarp,
and I see old Agnes
kneeling in the sand
beside me,

bony fingers grasping,
pulling.
We get the tarp through
so it's under
the dolphin's belly.

Everybody grab hold, I say,
and they do,
lifting the dolphin
in a tarp hammock
that I hope
is strong enough.
He's so heavy,
and his beautiful skin
is drying out.

More water, I yell,
and Mom and the sundress-lady
fill the containers again
and again
as we take tiny
careful
steps
into the sea.

I'm up to my knees—
so hard to hold on,
but he's lighter now.
Levi's across from me,
clenching his bit of blue tarp.

He catches my eye,
grinning,
and my heart lifts
in my chest
because that grin
means we did it,
or at least
almost...

We turn a half circle
so the dolphin
is facing away
from the beach,
wade out further
until I'm waist-deep
in the cold water.
The dolphin wiggles
like he's excited,
can barely wait
to swim again.
We lower the sides
of the tarp,
and he starts bobbing his head,
urging himself on,
the salt water of Felicity Bay
splashing our faces,
arms,
shirts,
and then
he's free.

A few seconds later
he turns back—
no no no!
We form a line,
a barrier,
all of us in the water
side by side,
arms stretched out,
holding hands
with the people beside us.
It's a message
the dolphin must understand,
because he turns again
and heads
out of the bay.
He leaps clear of the water,
and a cheer erupts,
all of us whooping
and my heart
pounding,
people clapping,
everyone laughing
with the pure joy of it.

The dolphin leaps again
then disappears
under the water,
but in that moment
before he vanishes,
I'm sure I see
a flash of turquoise
on his tail.

SALVATION

The lady next to me
grabs me in a hug
right there in the water.

You did it, Bailey!

She lets go and I realize
a sundress-lady
stood beside me,
got soaked,
joined hands
to save the dolphin.

I say, *You know my name?*

Of course, she says.
You're Marie's granddaughter.

She tells me
her name's Camellia,
and I wish
I'd known her name sooner.

Thanks for helping, I say,
and then I remember
banging on her door,
hollering at her,
and my cheeks burn.
I can't believe
I yelled,
commanded,
told adults
what to do.
I only knew
we had to save
the dolphin.

Well, you were right,
Camellia says.
When someone needs help,
a real community
pitches in.

Mom finds me,
wades through the water
with Nana Marie,
and they both hug me,
huge smiles plastered
on their faces.

That was amazing! Mom says.

We saved
a dolphin's life, I say,
and it almost
doesn't seem real.

You *saved him*, Nana Marie says,
but that's not all you did…look!

So many people
in the water,
on the beach,
wet and sandy,
clapping each other
on the back;
Jasper and the petition lady
chatting and smiling;
everyone happy
together.

Chickadee, says Nana Marie,
I haven't seen this town
so united over anything
in a good few years.

Nana Marie's words collide
with Jasper's prophecy—
'*saving the life of one*
will save the souls of many'—

and the truth of it all
fills me up,
expanding like a balloon
inside me.

All this time
I wanted to believe,
tried to believe,
yet part of me must've always
doubted,
or the truth wouldn't feel
like such a surprise—
a rogue wave
rising out of nowhere
and washing
over me.

Nana Marie puts her arm
around me,
other arm around Mom,
and the three of us
slosh back to the beach,
stroll across the sand
to where Kevin and Levi
are folding the tattered tarp.

I wish Daniel was here,
wish he could've seen the dolphin,
helped with the rescue,
felt the magic
of it all.

Gonna need a new tarp
for the tree house, Levi says,

and I realize
Daniel *did* help,
even though he doesn't
know it yet.

I can't wait
to tell him.

Bailey: I know you've gone back to the sea, but I'm leaving tomorrow. I just wanted to say good bye.

OLOTB: …

Bailey: I guess it's crazy to talk to an empty spot on the beach, isn't it?

OLOTB: …

Bailey: Then again, I guess you're somewhere, so maybe it's not crazy.

OLOTB: …

Bailey: I sort of feel like a superhero, you know. Not that it was all me—it was everyone pulling together, and I still think you had a little something to do with it, too, and the sea—they all went back in the sea!

OLOTB: …

Bailey: Can I tell you a secret? For a minute this afternoon, I thought the dolphin was you.

OLOTB: …

Bailey: It was definitely a dolphin, though. Right?

OLOTB: …

LETTING GO

Tuesday morning I wake
to golden light,
gulls squawking,
sea breeze dancing
with the curtains.
Something
doesn't seem right.
I climb down
off my bunk,
go to the bedroom window,
peer out—
blue sky,
beach,
ocean—
and I realize
what's different:
it's Tuesday,
but it's not
raining.

Kevin's voice
comes from the bottom bunk:

Is it high tide?

Yeah, I say. *Why?*

He throws back the covers.

There's something
I wanna do.

Now?

Yes! Come with me.

We get dressed,
go out through the kitchen
where Nana Marie
is stirring pancake batter.

Be back soon, she says
as we dash off.

Kevin leads me along the trail
to Arbutus Point
where the rope swing
hangs,
end hooked over a branch
for easy reaching.

What are we doing here, Kev?

He slips off his runners,
takes hold
of the rope,
fear
written all over his face.
He doesn't say anything,
just stands
at the edge
of the bluff,
holding the rope,
looking down,
blue water sparkling
in the morning sun.

I'm about to tell him
it's okay if he's scared,
about to tell him
he doesn't have to do this—
I'm certainly
not going to do it—
but then…

He jumps—
up,
out,
legs wrapping
around the rope,
swinging
and
screaming,
screaming

and
swinging,
until
he lets go,
drops,
sinks,
probably still screaming
under water.

He pops back up,
swims to shore
in a flurry
of splashing,
runs up the steep trail
back to me,
grinning like mad.

That was amazing, I say.
Way to go, Kev!

Then I ask him
if he's going to do it
again.
He shakes his head.

Don't need to, he says.

I guess you never know
how brave you are
until you let go
of the rope.

EVERYDAY MIRACLES

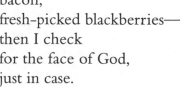

We clasp hands
around the table—
Mom, Nana Marie, Kevin, me.
Joined together like that
I feel Dad's absence
so strongly
it's almost as if
he's here,
which is very weird.
I let Kev's hand go,
keep mine outstretched,
ready to be grasped,
so Dad knows
there's a place for him.

Nana Marie asks a blessing
over the food—
pancakes,
bacon,
fresh-picked blackberries—
then I check
for the face of God,
just in case.

Anything? asks Mom.

I shake my head,
douse my plate with syrup,
dig in
to the sweet,
maple
goodness.

Someone knocks
on the kitchen door,
and a tiny hope
buried deep
wonders
if it's my dad,
even though Mom said
he'll meet us back home.

I excuse myself,
rush to the door,
fling it open.

It's not Dad.
Of course
it's not.

It's Daniel.

He looks
great—
pink cheeks,
goofy grin,
like he's not sick,
not
dying,
and I'm so relieved
I throw my arms around him
in a hug.
He laughs,
pulls back.

Nice to see you, too, he says.

Are you okay?

*Yeah. Gotta take extra
antibiotics for a while,
but I'm okay.*

He hands me a book—
paperback cover
with a picture
of the bay.
I flip through,
find picture
after picture
from my month
in Felicity Bay,

all those
beep
click
beep
times that Daniel
captured,
put in a book—
a baby crab,
mermaid hair,
Froot Loops,
sandy toes,
tree house,
and even
stained glass windows,
and a chalice—
moments
of significance,
ordinary things
that turned out to be
extraordinary.

I made it for you
on my mom's laptop,
he says. *Helped me pass the time*
in the hospital.

Thanks, I say. *I love it.*

Taped inside the back cover
is my rain-splattered picture
of Mom and Dad.
It's a bit warped
and wrinkled
from the dampness,
but I'm still glad
to have it.

Daniel fishes around
in his pocket,
hands me a crumpled bit
of paper.

> *My email,* he says
> nodding at the paper,
> *and cell. Text me sometime,*
> *okay?*

I realize
this is goodbye,
don't want to cry,
so I nod,
close my fingers
around the paper,
hold tight.

A DIFFERENT KIND OF PERFECT

All our stuff is loaded
in the car
when a half bicycle,
half freezer
appears in the lane.
Jasper rides up,
stops beside me,
smiles.

You're staying? I ask.

For now, he says, *but you're
leaving?*

Even though a month ago
I was a stranger,
wasn't even sure I wanted to come
to Felicity Bay,
now I know
I'll miss it terribly.
I nod at Jasper.

*We're catching
the next ferry.*

I'm glad to have met you, he says.
*I hope you come back
sometime.*

I hope so, too.

Jasper opens the freezer,
hands Kevin a Fudgsicle,
me an orange Creamsicle—
our favorites.

He says, *Have faith,*
gets back on his bike,
foot poised
on the pedal,
and looks hard at me.

I didn't know, he says.
Not at first.

Didn't know what? I say.

*That the stranger
would turn out to be you.
But I'm glad it did.*

He raises a hand
in a farewell salute.
Then he's gone.

Mom and Nana Marie
finish their goodbyes—
hugs and tears—
then Nana Marie
gathers up Kev and me,
kisses us both.

> *See you next summer,* Kev says,
> then he yells, *Shotgun!*
> and runs for the front seat.

He can ride up front—
I'd rather have another minute
with Nana Marie.
She whispers in my ear.

> *You gave me back a family, Chickadee.*

I can't say anything,
but I hug her
extra long.

We drive away from Felicity Bay,
windows down,
sea air whipping my hair
into tangles.
So much changed this summer.

Some of it
was because of me,
the stranger
from the sea.

When the ferry
pulls away from the dock,
engines roaring,
white foam churning,
I get out of the car,
go to the front,
and watch home
get closer.
It'll be weird
without Dad there,
can't imagine
it ever feeling right,
but he's still my dad
and now
I have Nana Marie, too—
a bigger family
than I had before.

I really thought I wanted magic—
for God to do big
dramatic
miracles,
fix my family,
Daniel's lungs,
everything,

but the ordinary mess
and the spoon-worthy,
beep-click-beep moments
are actually
sort of cool—
a different kind
of perfect.

Maybe I really can see
the face of God.
Maybe it's there
when I sit with my
patched-together family
for pancake breakfast.
Maybe it's in the power
of the sea,
or in the driftwood
that gets hurled about
by storms.
Maybe it's in the words
of an ice-cream man
or the joyful leaps
of a dolphin.
It might even be in the pain
of leaving my new best friend,
or maybe
it's especially in that.

Maybe all these things
show me the face of God,
or maybe they just show me
a bit of light
or love
or happiness.
And maybe that's exactly
the same thing.

I go to the back of the ferry,
Arbutus Island fading
into the distance,
and wave madly.

> *I'll be back,* I yell
> into the wind.

I close my hand
around the bit of turquoise sea glass
in my pocket,
rub its smooth edges
with my thumb—
a broken bit
made smooth and beautiful,
changed
by the sea.

Acknowledgments

My sincere thanks to everyone who helped me bring Bailey's story from rough draft to finished book. Special thanks to the River Writers—Kristin Butcher, Sheena Gnos, Jocelyn Reekie, Janet Smith, Diana Stevan, and Liezl Sullivan; my critique partners, Catherine Knutsson and Beth Smith; *Pitch Wars* mentor Stefanie Wass; beta readers kc dyer and Carol Garvin; my editor, Ann Featherstone, and the fantastic team at Pajama Press. Thanks also to the members of the *Pitch Wars* 2014 Facebook group for their cheerleading and TLC, and to all who have supported and encouraged me.

Thank you to Chris Black, for reading the manuscript and answering questions about CF, and to the Vancouver Aquarium Marine Mammal Rescue Centre, for answering my questions about dolphin behavior and rescue. Any errors are my own.

Finally and especially, thank you to my precious family, for always handling my dreams with care.